BY THE BOOK

Make Me A Match

KAY LYONS

BY THE BOOK

Chapter 1

"Tommy, come on," Claire Simmons called to her thirteen-year-old son. "I'd like to get there *today*."

"So go," Tommy said, his reply muffled by the door.

She knocked softly and opened the wooden panel. "We are not doing this. You are in so much trouble right now after getting suspended. I hated calling Grandpa to cancel last minute because of you doing your punishment at the school, but I made excuses for y— Scott Thomas Simmons, you haven't even *packed*?"

Her son lifted a bony shoulder in reply and glared at her, his six-foot frame sprawled out on the bed with his feet hanging over the side.

"I don't want to *go*," he said, drawing out the words.

Claire inhaled and dug to the very edges of her soul for patience. "We are surprising Grandpa and spending a fabulous few weeks at the beach while I polish my resume and apply for jobs. Pack."

The day after Tommy's end-of-year detention and makeups, she'd showed up at work like so many others only to be called into a group meeting in the conference room and told to gather her things, handed an envelope, and escorted from the building.

Reeling from the sudden job loss, she'd sat down and taken a hard look at her finances, Tommy's behavior, and her reasons for staying in Virginia Beach after Scott's death rather than moving back to Carolina Cove.

Her father was well and able-bodied now, but there would come a point where he'd need help, and she didn't want to be six hours away like she'd been when her mother had collapsed and died from a heart attack before she could make it to see her.

There was also the fact things had been so strained between her and her father since her pregnancy at seventeen, and after losing her mother, Claire didn't want that to be the case with her only living parent.

What better time than now to reconnect with her father and check out the job market there, but also take a much-needed vacation while trying to get Tommy on a more even keel since his father's death?

Sounds like a lot to pack into a short stay.

"Do I have to?"

Really? What kid *didn't* want to go to the beach? "Yes, you have to. *Now*—or you go without clothes or shoes or anything else for the foreseeable future with only yourself to blame. You have thirty minutes to gather your stuff and meet me at the door. And do not leave your room a mess— I *will* check. Your bed is to be made, drawers and closet closed, and floor cleaned up before you leave this room. Understood?"

"I don't want to sell our house! I don't want to leave my friends."

"Your so-called *friends* got you suspended for a *third* time. You're lucky the principal had mercy and let you take the tests to advance with your class."

"This is our house. *Dad's* house," Tommy muttered, glaring at her with tears in his yes, so like his father's.

The impact shredded her insides but she stood firm. She wasn't sure she *wanted* to move, either, but with the market as hot as it was, her only immediate male family too far away to lend a helping hand and give Tommy the guidance he obviously needed, and her job now nonexistent, the timing couldn't be ignored. Maybe even considered a sign? "I haven't made a firm decision of whether we'll move or not, but Miss Cynthia is coming over while we're gone to look around and see what she thinks she can price the house for. She may even have a couple of people interested enough to make offers."

"I don't *care*!"

"Well, I do. And whether we move to Carolina Cove or stay in Virginia, this house is way more than I can afford on my own. I'm going to talk to Grandpa about it once we get there because he's good at these kinds of decisions, but in the meantime…Tommy, I need a break, okay? A vacation and time to clear my head and destress from everything that's going on and… now's the best time, while I'm between jobs. Help me out here. *Please*."

Claire waited for him to grudgingly get to his feet and grab a duffle bag before she left the room so as to not hear his mutterings.

Outside his door, she ran through her mental checklist one last time as she wandered the house. Garage door closed, house looking good for her Realtor friend. What else?

Mail—her neighbor would also get the mail and let her know if anything important showed up.

Her bills were on autopay to get the discounts available for doing so and could be accessed from her laptop… That was everything.

So, why did it feel like she was missing something?

You say that every time we go anywhere.

With a hard tug at her heartstrings, Scott's voice sounded in her mind, and she closed her eyes, reveling in the memory of him standing by the door, hand on the knob, looking amused and amazingly patient while she tore through the house at the last minute, checking everything before whatever getaway they were taking.

Back then it was typically short weekend trips or the occasional vacation if the timing had worked out with his deployment schedule, but now…

Her gaze settled on a photo and Claire walked to the sofa table. This was taken…three years ago?

Yeah, three. Before her mom's death and Tommy's growth spurt.

In the year since Scott's accident, the days had started to blur together in a rush of busy-ness, stress, and the numbness of grief. Losing Scott so soon after losing her mother…

She hadn't meant to ignore her father these last two years, but given the distance and her own inability to cope, plus Tommy, her job, and just trying to keep her head above water long enough to take a breath, she was sure her father felt that way.

And probably angrier because of it.

Claire carried the frame to her computer bag and carefully tucked it inside to take with her.

That done, she turned to run through that checklist again. Scott's death benefits had allowed her to pay down a lot of their debt but not all, and she'd be lying if she said she wasn't panicking now due to her job loss.

She'd loved her husband with every fiber of her being, but he sucked when it came to money and self-gratification. Things that should've been done—paid—weren't.

Like the life insurance she thought was being carried through the military that had been cancelled without her being aware.

Being a single mom while Scott was deployed, working, and handling things at home meant sometimes things slipped by her.

But it was the over-the-top extras that got them. Scott liked big, expensive toys like boats and trucks and Harleys, and he'd constantly rolled from one model into a bigger, supposedly better one. That meant when the time had come to sell the toys, she hadn't been able to get anywhere near the amounts financed on them.

Then there were the homes they'd purchased because Scott didn't like living on base. They'd racked up some serious craziness when it was time to pack up and move again. They got a housing stipend, but it took time to sell homes, and money.

Before moving to Virginia, they'd had trouble selling two of the homes they'd purchased during previous moves, and they'd carried mortgages and rental expenses until they'd been able to unload them both at losses.

Because of the heavy debt, the benefits she'd received hadn't been enough to cover everything. She still had a mortgage on their current house, but it had built up quite a bit of equity as the real estate prices in the area had soared in the last year or so.

Her biggest regret in light of Tommy's nefarious activities was that maybe she should've taken more time off of work after Scott's passing. But with Tommy back in school during the day and their monthly bills still to pay, the thought of wandering the house with nothing to occupy her mind left her desperate for the hours she'd spent at her job.

Now she was income-less due to cutbacks, Tommy was

acting out worse by the day, and her last phone call with her father in Carolina Cove had been sad.

They'd sat there in silence, phones to their ears, nothing to say once the how are yous were out of the way.

That wasn't the way things should be. She knew enough to know that.

He'd seemed lonely, talked only about work, and she hated that it had been so long since their last visit, even though her mother had been the glue that kept them speaking.

A door slammed in the hallway behind her, and she turned to find Tommy trudging toward her with a duffle, two backpacks, his gym bag, and tote with wires dragging behind. "You went into my closet? No video games is part of your punishment."

"I want to take them if we're there longer than you think."

"Tommy…you broke into the school and vandalized it. They were talking about prosecuting all of you. You got off easy just having to do cleanup."

"I know. I won't play them. I'm taking them just in case."

"Fine. We'll pack them *but* I keep them with me in my room."

"Whatever."

"What was that?"

"Nothing. Do I *have to*—"

"Yes," she said, quickly moving to open the door. "Do I need to check your room?"

"No. I cleaned it up."

"Thank you. Here we go." Any beach items they'd need would be in her father's garage. Chairs, bodyboards, surfboards, etc.

She grabbed the last of her stuff to be loaded and

wondered how minimalists did it. Because truth be told, Tommy got his packing skills from her. Had they actually had to pack beach items, she would've needed a van. Or the truck she'd sold a month after Scott's passing when the almost-thousand-dollar-a-month payment had come due.

While Tommy put the last of their belongings in the Wrangler, she returned to the house to make sure nothing had been left behind—as well as take a quick look in Tommy's room—before locking up and climbing behind the wheel.

Tommy sat next to her in the seat, looking every bit as disgruntled and gloomy as ever. "Why don't you pick out some good music for us?"

Her moody son rolled his eyes and pulled out his earphones to place on his head, shutting out the world and her with it.

Chapter 2

Almost six hours later, they crossed the Snow's Cut Bridge and kept going to Carolina Cove.

During the long drive, she'd made a mental list of fun things to do that Tommy might like.

She thought they could take the top and doors off the Jeep and drive out on the beach to fish. Go visit the *USS North Carolina* battleship moored in downtown Wilmington. Rent Jet Skis. Maybe take the ferry to Bald Head Island and get a golf cart for the day to explore?

Anything that might possibly reverse the sour frown permanently marring her son's face of late.

She made the turns leading to her parents' home and pulled into the drive, ready for a long stretch and walk on the beach to clear her head and help her figure out a plan for the future now that she was jobless.

She had a small savings and a severance package, which would help cover expenses short-term, but finding a new job was paramount. "Hey," she said to Tommy. "I'm sure Grandpa's *really* missed you, so don't be rolling your eyes or giving him attitude. Got it?"

"Whatever."

She fought her urge to roll her own eyes at her son's mood and got out of the Wrangler, noting the strange vehicle in the driveway. "Let's take a load up to the apartment as we go," she ordered, opening the rear door to hand off bags to her grumpy son.

She found the right key before loading up and making her way to the stairs beside the garage. "Tommy? Are you coming?"

"Get the door open first," Tommy said with a grumble. "There's nowhere to stand up there."

The landing at the top of the stairs *was* narrow, but she doubted that was his reasoning. Lately Tommy was dead set against anything he deemed she wanted. Blue was green, wrong was right, and nothing made him happy. But how much of it was typical teen hormones and how much of it mourning for his father?

Sweating, huffing, and straining beneath the weight of the multiple bags she carried, she dropped what was in her right hand and removed the key ring she'd held in her mouth for the trudge up the stairs.

She tried the key but it didn't fit—maybe because the lock looked brand-new?

Salt air did a lot of damage to such things, so it was little surprise that it had needed to be changed since their last trip two years ago. Still—

The door opened with a yank, and she stepped back, unbalanced by the bags and the surprise of the half-naked man on the other side. A man who quickly reached out and grabbed her by the shoulders to keep her from tumbling backward over the railing, weighted down by luggage.

She blinked, eyes flaring when she took in his wet skin, the damp towel around his slim and tightly honed waist, and a muscle-ripped chest that would've looked like something out of *GQ* if not for the bruises and scars.

Was that a *gunshot* wound?

Scott had had one from his first tour, and the two looked the same.

"Can I help you?"

"Uh…"

The man raised an eyebrow and released his grip on her shoulders, a pained expression flashing over his features as he lowered his injured arm.

"You hurt yourself grabbing me," she said, her gazing shifting to his shoulder to keep from looking into brown eyes that seemed to bore into her soul.

"It's fine."

"Mom, come on. What's the deal?" Tommy called from below.

The man crossed his arms over his chest, but she noted it was probably more to cradle and relieve the pain of his injured arm. "Uh, I'm not sure," she said, shifting her gaze to the man once again. Considering he stood there in nothing but a towel, it was hard to focus. "I'm Claire Simmons. My father owns the house and… Who are you?"

"Marcus Denz," he said. "I'm his renter."

"Claire?" her father called from the bottom of the stairs. "What are you doing here?"

"What are we… Dad, you said the apartment was free. That you weren't renting it out this summer."

"Changed my mind. That's Denz," her father said, pointing at the man drying in the afternoon sun.

"We've met," she said, feeling flushed from the fact she could smell the scent of his clean skin, something musky with a touch of sandalwood.

"You should've called," her father said, shuffling his sandaled feet and squinting up at her. "Apartment's taken."

"Yeah, I see that. Surprise," she said, forcing a grin. "You're right, I should've called. But I didn't and…now we're here. Is it, um, okay if we stay in the house with you?"

"That's fine," her father said.

Claire opened her mouth only to close it again. Obviously reminding her father that she'd told him they *were* coming to visit as soon as they could that summer wouldn't do her any good now.

"I should get dressed. Leave the bags and I'll help you," the man said.

She gripped the key in her hand so tightly that the edges dug into her skin, but she managed a smile. "None needed. Thanks."

That said, she ignored the man in all his towel-wearing gorgeousness and snagged the bag she'd dropped while trying to open the door before trudging back down the rickety staircase to where her father and son waited. After a round of painfully awkward hugs, Big Tom, as her mother had always called him once Tommy had come along, gathered up the bags she'd set down and turned toward the house.

"I thought you'd decided not to rent the apartment anymore after having so much trouble with the last tenant," she murmured.

"Didn't plan to but Denz isn't like that guy."

"Oh? Where did you meet him?"

"Fishing. I helped him reel in a shark last weekend."

She stopped walking and stared at her father's shoulders. "But you did a background check, right? A credit check? *Any* kind of check?"

Her father paused with his hand on the back door and shot her a look over his shoulder. "Denz is good people and we have a short-term lease. That's all I need to know."

Tom entered the house and kept going, and Claire paused to allow Tommy to enter in front of her.

She turned to stare up at the apartment door in time to see it close.

The man sported a gunshot wound.

The question was why?

Chapter 3

Denz watched as Claire Simmons practically sprinted down the rickety stairs after her father. Sensing he was being studied, he turned and found the kid staring up at him, a deep frown on the boy's glowering face.

Denz raised an eyebrow in the kid's direction, which the boy ignored. The trio moved toward the back of Tom's one-level home, their voices so low Denz couldn't hear what was being said.

He stepped back into the apartment and shut the door, wincing when he bumped his shoulder against the narrow doorframe. He needed to check around and find a trainer familiar with PT for such injuries, something he'd promised his doc he'd do the moment he'd arrived.

He'd put it off, thinking the exercises he did on his own would be enough, but obviously that wasn't the case given the way his shoulder had stiffened up after fishing off the pier. Maybe he had briefly wrangled a shark, but four days later, he was still paying for it. Not a good sign.

He walked toward the small bedroom.

The sixty-something man had noticed Denz struggling

to fish one-handed and helped reel in the four-foot shark. They'd celebrated over lunch at the nearby diner, and they discovered both worked within the Wilmington film industry. That's when Tom mentioned having an apartment to rent.

Denz got dressed and left the apartment in time to see Claire walking toward her Jeep. He met her at the rear of the vehicle and silently offered a hand, which she eyed like a snake.

"Thanks. But I have it."

"Just being polite, seeing as how I apparently took your apartment."

He watched as she squinted up at him, her blue eyes the color of a dark sky. "I had to cancel on him a few weeks ago but told him we'd be coming soon. It's fine. We'll make it work."

"The offer stands," he said, indicating the bags.

Her full pink lips twisted in a semblance of a smile.

"Fine. But nothing with your bad arm. I don't want to be held responsible if you reinjure it."

"Roger that."

Claire froze in the act of pulling a duffle from the back of the Wrangler. "You're military?"

"Used to be."

"So you were medically discharged after being shot?"

Her gaze dropped to his shoulder and the sling he now wore. "I left the military five years ago."

"Oh. I-I… You're a cop?"

"Bodyguard." He reached out and grabbed the duffle, sliding it to his good shoulder. "You planning on staying a while?" If she wanted answers, maybe she ought to answer a few questions herself.

Claire side-eyed him as she grabbed another bag.

"I haven't decided yet."

He grabbed another bag.

"No, leave that. It's Tommy's. He can unload his own."

He frowned, noting the tote bag full of gaming equipment she held. "But that's yours?" he asked, indicating the tote.

"For now. Tommy's grounded," she said, "and gaming is off-limits. But since we weren't sure how long we're staying, he asked if he could bring it just in case."

"Smart kid."

"Yeah, well, it stays with me."

Denz followed her to the back door of the house and inside.

"Tommy, go get your stuff," she called.

"Grandpa said I had to help him," Tommy said from somewhere in the house.

Denz paused behind Claire as she stalled just inside a bedroom, watching as the kid tried to place a fitted sheet on the mattress only to discover it was too short.

A four-letter word escaped his mouth and earned a gasp from Claire. "*Scott Thomas.*"

"It slipped."

"Not acceptable," she said, shifting toward the left to drop the bags beside the wall opposite the bed.

"I can't even keep it in my room?" the kid asked, eyeing the bag with the game system.

"What do you think?"

The kid grumbled, yanking the sheet so hard Denz waited for it to rip.

"Here we go," Tom said, coming into the small bedroom behind Denz. The man eyed Denz and the bags he carried before tossing the additional linens on the bed. "Try those. I think the ones you have are for your bed in the other room."

Thankfully Tom missed the look that flashed over the

kid's expression at the mix-up, but Denz met the kid's gaze and held it until the kid looked away.

Denz had only known Tom a matter of days, but he was a decent man, one who didn't need disrespecting by his grandson.

"Denz, put those down before you rip those stitches," Tom said. "Denz here is a bodyguard. He's worked with some of the celebrities here in town."

"I'm going to my room," Tommy said.

"Make your bed," Tom said. "Don't make your mama come do it for you."

Denz met the kid's gaze as he passed by and caught another flash of anger. The kid was a walking powder keg.

"I see," Claire said, her tone measured, as though she didn't quite believe it.

"It's not a bad gig," he told her. "I get to travel, and the pay is good."

"It ought to be if getting shot is in the job description," Claire said dryly, glancing at him before focusing on the tote bag remaining in her hand.

She shoved that one into the closet and tossed another bag on top as though trying to hide it.

"He may have caught a bullet but he saved a life," Tom said.

"I did my job," Denz corrected.

"And you obviously did right by it since the guy's walking around today," Tom said, sliding a quelling look at his daughter.

Denz took a step back, not wanting to participate in the tension he felt in the room. "Well, I'm going to head out," he said to Tom. "You folks enjoy your evening."

"Thanks for the help," Tom said.

"Yes, thank you," Claire added.

Denz walked out of the bedroom when he heard Tom speak.

"Don't you be giving Denz a hard time," Tom said.

"I wasn't."

"You were," Tom said.

"I simply asked about his profession."

"Well, now you know."

"Dad—"

"Why are you here, Claire?"

Denz paused in the hallway and waited to hear her response.

"I thought you wanted us to visit. Is that not okay? If not, we can go."

Okay then. No tension there.

Tom mumbled something in his gruff voice as Denz walked away.

Chapter 4

Claire yanked the sheets apart and began making the bed, aware of her father watching her every move.

"You're here. Might as well stay."

Oh, that was a welcome, wasn't it? "I told you we were coming to visit, Dad."

"And then you cancelled."

"Something came up but I said we'd come soon."

"I saw on the news where your company fired people. You one of them?"

She inhaled and ran a hand through her shoulder-length hair, wishing the world wasn't as connected as it was nowadays. "Yeah, I am. They sold out and made cutbacks. I got a small severance."

Her father pursed his lips and made a grumbling noise.

"Been a year since Scott's death, too."

Did her father have to be so in tune with *everything*?

"Military housing money dried up, didn't it? That's some bad timing," he continued, even though she hadn't answered.

"I'm just here to regroup while I get my resume in

order and put in some applications." She'd wanted to talk to her dad about selling her house but now wasn't the time. Especially not when he was in one of his anti-Scott moods. "Tommy and I both needed a break, and we hadn't been back to visit for a-a while, so I thought we'd come to the beach…and visit."

Her father watched her as she smoothed the bedsheet before moving to the opposite side.

"Boy's grown a full foot since last I saw him."

Glad for the change in topic, she nodded. "Tommy's a bottomless pit, too. I actually caught him eating sardines straight from the tin one day because I hadn't gone to the grocery store."

"That's disgusting."

She laughed, knowing full well her father's take on them. "I couldn't agree more." There, something they agreed on. Sardines were Scott's thing, though, and he'd loved them on pizza, as did Tommy. To her it was the most unappetizing thing ever, but to each his own.

"How'd he do in school this year? Still making good grades?" her father asked.

Finished with that side, she grabbed the flat sheet and began again. "Um, not entirely. He struggled this year, which isn't surprising given the circumstances. Tommy couldn't seem to find his groove. But he managed to move on with his class." *Barely*.

"It was that bad?"

If she wanted her father's help with Tommy during their stay, she knew she had to be honest with him. Too bad it couldn't have waited until after her beach walk and a little decompression time. "Yeah, it was." She ducked her head and made a show of palming the sheet perfectly smooth and tucking it quarter-bouncing tight.

"Maybe I can talk to the boy while you're here. See if I can talk some sense into him."

Talk some sense into him? She swallowed hard and nodded, hoping that was her father's way of being sympathetic rather than controlling. "He needs a good male role model," she said. "I think he misses that, you know? It's tough for a kid his age to only have his mom."

Awkward silence filled the room, and her father shuffled his feet in that way he always did when he was uncomfortable or his mind was on other things.

"Dad, I took it for granted that the apartment would be free and I shouldn't have. Thanks. For letting us stay with you."

"You think I'd kick you out? My own daughter and grandson?"

Hearing the rising tone in his voice, she hurried to deflate the tension. "No, of course not. I just meant… We've stayed in the apartment ever since Scott and I got married. Not in the house. I…don't want to intrude."

"This is your room. Always has been. You're the one who left it. By choice, I might add."

A trembling began deep inside of her when faced with the anger her father had toward her decision to marry so young. One would think, sometime over the years since, tensions would have eased, but they hadn't. "You and Denz seem to have formed a fast friendship over that shark."

"I suppose. Your mama always said men were strange that way, bonded over unusual things like war and fights and fishing," he said.

"Dad, I don't want to sound paranoid, but what do you know about him? I mean, that's obviously a bullet wound in his shoulder, so yeah, he's been shot, but are you *sure* that story about being a bodyguard is legit?"

"Why would he lie?"

"Oh, I don't know, maybe because he committed a crime? Is in a gang or a cartel?"

Her father's chuckles filled the small bedroom she'd used from her birth until she was seventeen and snuck out the window to run away with Scott.

"You've got quite the imagination."

"It's not such a leap these days, especially when you say you're always watching the news. Drug running, human trafficking… People get shot all the time. It's very possible. People lie." *Even husbands.*

Not that she'd admit that to her father.

"I got a copy of his license and a business card for the company he works for, and before you ask, yes, I called it. He's legit."

The air left her lungs in a rapid exhalation as relief poured in. She still didn't like the man's chosen profession —or any profession equating to danger—but at least her father didn't have a fugitive in the garage.

Bed made, she straightened and looked at the array of bags lining the wall and atop the chair. She should unpack before things got too wrinkled, but more than anything, she wanted some sand between her toes and salt air in her lungs. "I think I'm going to check on Tommy and go take a walk on the beach before I tackle those. I'll help with dinner when I get back. Or would you rather order something? Go out to eat?"

"I'll make something."

Her father loved to cook, which was why his food service business did so well. She might be a little biased, but she thought he made the best shrimp tacos on the East Coast.

Claire moved toward the door only to stop when her father cleared his throat.

She met his gaze and waited.

"Never mind."

"What did you want to say?"

"Nothing that can't wait. Go check on your boy and make sure he's not up to no good. I need to know if I need to nail his windows shut like I should have yours."

Claire lifted her chin, a hot rush of tears prickling her eyes to the point heavy blinking almost didn't do the trick. "I'm sorry for the embarrassment I caused you with my teenage pregnancy, but had it not happened, I wouldn't have Tommy and I'm *not* sorry about that, so if you think I should be…shame on you."

Chapter 5

Denz walked into Reels, a restaurant and bar near the marina, and quickly spied the group he'd come to meet.

"Denz!" Marsali Beck cried, her sweet voice full of welcome and a smile on her face.

"Hey, Mrs. B, how are you?"

"Are you ever going to call me Marsali?" she asked.

Denz shared a look with her movie star husband and shook his head. "No, ma'am. Mr. Beck, it's good to see you."

"You, too, Denz," Oliver said, shaking Denz's hand.

The table was filled with Marsali and Oliver's friends, including Marsali's brother and Reels' owner, Mac, and his beautiful new fiancée—a former ballet dancer from New York City turned ballet teacher and business owner here on the island last he'd heard.

"Sit, sit!" Marsali said. "It's weird to see you in an unofficial capacity. A good weird, though. You've been with us so much you're practically family."

He chuckled along with the rest of the group at Marsali's attempt to soften the weirdness comment. "I appreciate that. And I understand. When I ran into Mr. Beck on the street a few days ago, it seemed a little odd." He'd been exploring downtown Wilmington, walking along the sidewalk outside the Cotton Exchange building, when he'd stumbled onto a movie set.

He'd watched along with the crowd gathered while Oliver had sat in the director's chair and the actors did their thing. Once finished, Denz had grinned when Oliver did a double take on spotting him in the crowd.

After motioning him to come behind the barriers, Oliver had chatted him up and invited him to tonight's dinner.

"How's the shoulder?" Carter asked.

Marsali and Oliver's neighbor had his hand resting on the back of his wife's chair. Eliza looked preoccupied, no doubt thinking of a wedding plan in the works. Most probably for Mac and V, as Victoria liked to be called. "It's healing. Thanks for asking."

"Any idea when you'll be cleared for work?" Oliver asked.

"No. Not yet."

"What happened again?" Marsali asked. "I mean, Oliver said you were shot while working but…"

He smiled at the questions bombarding him. "Right place, wrong time. Or right time as the case may be."

"You got the guy?" Mac asked.

Denz nodded. "He's awaiting trial and everyone is safe."

"You know," Marsali said with her girl-next-door tone and sweet expression, "you'd have a lot easier time finding someone special if things like that weren't an everyday possibility."

"Watch out," Lincoln said.

"Here we go again," Carter said with a grin.

"Seriously, Marse, do you ever stop trying to match-make?" Eliza asked.

"She does have a point," Amelia added.

Denz lowered his head and chuckled at the friends' many comments and inputs on his life.

It was risky seeing them as anything more than acquaintances or associates, but given that he was off-duty and simply a guy meeting a former client for dinner, he tried to keep it in perspective. "I like what I do, Mrs. B. I'm good at it."

When Denz had first started working in Oliver's protection rotation, Amelia and Lincoln were the only ones coupled up.

As the months passed, the group grew as Marsali, a professional matchmaker, did her thing with Eliza and Carter. Not long after, Marsali had an on-air blunder and mistakenly told the world Oliver Beck was her perfect match.

The media storm had been intense, with Oliver flying to Carolina Cove to protect his best friend's little sister from the paparazzi. It wasn't long before the two fell in love and married last fall.

The last single of the group, Mac, had given in to Marsali's requests to match him last summer, and now Mac and V's wedding date grew closer by the day.

"I'm just saying," Marsali continued. "If Denz is going to be in town for a while until he heals, he might get lonely. I could match you up with a lovely—"

"No," he said firmly. He was a by-the-book kind of guy, and some boundaries were too personal to cross. Marsali setting him up was one of them. "Thanks, though, Mrs. B. I appreciate the offer, but like you said, most women don't particularly care for my profession or the travel and time it requires. My relationships tend to be…brief."

Marsali's freckled face and expression revealed her displeasure at his words, but it was the truth. He wouldn't be in town long enough to form an attachment, and if he did, it would end badly. Like Marsali said, women tended to want stability and presence, and he couldn't offer either at this point. Nor did he particularly want to.

There were people meant for houses and picket fences, roots. His belongings fit into a single duffle and suitcase that allowed him to travel the world at a moment's notice. Why put himself or the woman through that? That's why casual dating worked for him. A nice dinner or two, maybe some fun. He'd yet to meet a woman who made him want more than companionship with no strings.

"Where are you staying?" Lincoln asked.

"I found a rental on the island. A little garage apartment that suits my needs. The owner actually works in craft service," he stated, using Hollywood's term for caterer. According to Tom, his food truck made the rounds to wherever the filming took place, be it downtown outside of the small studio building or on location.

"Anyone interesting in the vicinity?" Marsali asked.

The question made him mentally picture Claire.

Marsali's eyes widened and a smile curled her lips.

"There *is*."

"Marsali, leave the poor guy alone," Oliver said. "Otherwise the next time his number is up for us, he won't take the assignment."

Guardian Group rotated their guards periodically with no warning. It was to keep guards and their charges from getting too close and forming intimate attachments. Spending so much time together in tense or downright dangerous situations had a tendency to remove barriers faster than normal, which could be dangerous for everyone involved if the guard lost his or her objectivity.

"Who is she?" Marsali asked.

Denz glanced at her husband, who shrugged.

"You know she's like a dog with a bone."

"A dog? Really?" Marsali shot a tolerating glare at her SO. "I'd better be a cute one."

"Always."

Denz watched the byplay with amusement. "I never said there was a she, Mrs. B."

"You didn't have to. I'm good at reading people, and while you do a really good stone-cold, tough-guy expression, you slipped and I saw it. Now, who is she?"

Carter, Lincoln, and Mac as well as the ladies drilled him with their gazes. "Okay, fine. There may have been a surprise today."

"Oh, do tell," Marsali said, sliding an elbow onto the table to prop her chin on, waiting expectantly.

He shook his head at her antics. "The, uh, guy I rented the apartment from has a daughter and grandson who showed up to visit."

"Oh, do you know anything else about her? How old is her son?" Marsali asked.

"I'd guess fifteen given his height, but I think he's younger. Big kid, though. Needs to be in basketball."

"Not married?" Marsali's eyes lit up like a Christmas tree.

"Couldn't tell you," he said.

"Was she wearing a ring?"

"Mrs. B, stop."

Everyone laughed.

"I haven't done anything," she said, blinking innocently.

"You're thinking it and…trust me, she'd say no. She had a lot to say about the fact I've got a bullet wound."

"How'd she see it and know the sling wasn't for a broken arm or something?" Eliza asked.

Realizing he'd dug himself a hole he was going to have to climb out of, he grabbed the water glass in front of him and wished the waitress would hurry up. "I'd just gotten out of the shower when I heard someone trying to get into the apartment. The owner had said people sometimes walk through the yards on their way to the beach just to see what they can steal, so I opened the door."

"*Naked?*" Marsali asked, gasping.

Denz was well aware of the glares he was now receiving from the ladies' male companions. "I had a towel."

"Mmm, but where?" Eliza, the most ornery one in the group, murmured with a blink and a grin.

Eliza's husband whispered something in her ear, and she waggled her eyebrows at him, eyes sparkling and a flirtatious look on her face.

"I was perfectly respectable considering I thought someone was breaking in," he countered. Were all women like this? He hadn't been around many in a setting like this one, but the questions had him squirming in his seat, something his boss wouldn't be happy to see.

"Are you ready to order?" the waitress asked, finally pausing by their table.

Denz stared up at the teenager like the lifeline she was. "Definitely."

"We've got his," Marsali said to the waitress. "It's a business meeting, after all."

Denz's fingers gripped the menu until his fingers turned white. "I am not joining your database, Mrs. B."

Marsali gave him the sweetest smile and cocked her head to one side.

"Hmm. Are you sure about that?"

Chapter 6

Claire left the house after her statement to her father about Tommy and hurried down the streets toward the ocean.

She reveled in the sand between her toes and the sound of the seagulls squawking overhead. Claire walked for quite a while, every step and breath an attempt to free herself of the anxiety and upset she carried.

She spotted shells and sea glass and shark teeth along her path but left them for someone else to find. They weren't the treasures she searched for. No, what she desired was peace, guidance, and the discernment needed to know what to do next. Especially when it was abundantly clear her father still harbored more than his share of animosity and upset with her and her decisions.

After a while, she moved closer to the surf, drawn to it as she'd always been. There was just something about the ebb and flow of the water over her feet, the way her weight sank as the wave rolled back yet she stayed firmly in place.

She liked that feeling and let it happen a few more times until the sand anchored her. It wasn't until then that she let go of the breath she didn't know she'd been holding, the kind that came from deep within and shuddered on the way out.

If she focused on the fear building inside of her, panic followed shortly thereafter. So she focused on the moment, on breathing, counting as she inhaled, held, and released several breaths.

It would be okay. Things would work out exactly as they were meant to. Everything would be fine.

It had been quite a while since her last trip to the beach. Funny how those who lived so close wound up too busy to enjoy the very location they worked so hard to live by.

Since she'd grown up here, then lived all over the US before being sent to Virginia Beach, one would think it would be a given that the beach was a daily occurrence, but life seemed to always interfere.

First it was military life as a very young, very new wife with a baby on the way. Then an infant during a first deployment and the adjustments that had to be made as a single parent. Time passed quickly with that kind of busyness, and over the years and three tours, a lot of it was a blur.

A bigger wave headed her way, drawing her out of her pensiveness, and Claire braced herself, smiling when it made her lose her balance, and she wobbled with her feet entrenched in the sand. She tried pulling one foot out, but she was deep enough now that it was like wearing concrete shoes.

A broad hand appeared and gently latched on to her elbow. Claire gasped, lifting her head to find Denz staring down at her, looking every bit as handsome as he had earlier when he'd left for his dinner.

This time, however, he was dressed in running shorts,

shoes, and a sleeveless shirt. Probably to cover the scars and bruising and not draw attention.

Staring up at him now, she realized his hair was a dark brown, not the black she'd thought it was when standing in the doorway wet, and his brown eyes were mahogany streaked with gold, rather than plain, boring brown.

"Still stuck?"

What? Oh.

She hurried to pull her feet from their sandy prison and stepped up out of the hole where she'd sunk. "Thanks."

"No problem. How far did you plan on sinking?"

She shrugged. "If I'd had shorts on instead of capris, maybe a little more. How was your, um, dinner?"

Was it weird to ask a total stranger about his plans? It wasn't like they had a connection other than two brief meetings earlier today.

"It was nice."

"Oh?" Marcus Denz didn't seem to be much of a talker, but then men in his line of work typically weren't. Discretion was everything, and they tended to be guys who kept their emotions to themselves and suffered whatever the consequences of doing so.

Scott was the same, never sharing much of what he'd experienced during combat. Still, the nightmares and almost desperate spending to have nice things because, according to him, you only lived once, told her a lot in hindsight.

She wondered sometimes if Scott felt he had to live for the buddies he'd lost, the spending an outlet to get whatever he could while he was there to enjoy it. "Did it have anything to do with you being a bodyguard?" she asked, forcing herself to focus on something else.

"Yeah, actually, it did. Off and on over the last year

and a half I've guarded a Hollywood celebrity. He's a good guy and he's settled in the area with his wife."

"Oh, my word, you know *Oliver Beck*?" she cried, gaping up at him because she just couldn't help it. "That's who you mean, isn't it? He married a girl I went to school with, and they live here and... *That's* who you had dinner with tonight?"

He chuckled at her excitement but she couldn't help it. She was a total fangirl. Always had been. Every girl in school had crushed on Marsali's brother, Mac, and his college roommate, Oliver.

Claire had lost touch with high school friends once she'd gotten pregnant and married, but she'd gobbled up every news bite she could find about Marsali and Oliver's romance in the last year.

Oliver Beck could actually act, and he looked good doing it. Throw in his down-to-earth personality, his rise to stardom, and him choosing Marsali over Hollywood, and what wasn't to like? He was America's golden boy and he'd married a Carolina sweetheart in a wedding still being talked about.

"Uh, it is. As well as some of their friends."

"I have Marsali's book on dating. I haven't read it yet because, well, I'm *not*, but...I have it. For when I am, I mean."

Yeah, that long-winded ramble ended awkwardly. But Denz seemed to take it in stride.

"Mrs. B has some good advice in there, especially the part about dating safety."

"You've read it?"

Since it was a dating guide specifically aimed for good girls, she couldn't help her surprise.

"Figured I should, all things considered."

"Why do you say it like that?" she asked, catching a note of…something. Even though she wasn't sure what.

"Like what?"

"You had a tone."

"I didn't have a tone."

"You did. Okay, fine," she said when his expression hardened a bit and she was afraid he'd clam up. "No tone. But what did you mean by the tone you didn't have?"

She watched as his eyebrows formed a deep V as though he either struggled to keep a straight face or debated what or how much to say.

"Mrs. B is a really nice woman. But nice, sweet people tend to make easy targets, so I read it to see how much personal information she might have inadvertently included."

"Oooh. I see. I hadn't thought of it that way but it makes total sense. Is that why Oliver hired security for her?"

"I can't speculate on his reasons."

"Of course. I understand. I mean, with Carolina Cove being a tourist town, it leaves him open to constantly being seen and approached by locals *and* all of the visitors, which means going anywhere could be a huge hassle. Add Marsali's growing popularity… Have they had issues while being here? Security issues?"

Silence followed her words and she bit her lip. "You can't give specifics."

"Right."

"Got it," she said, squinting up at him since the sun was behind him. "Still, it's cool that you know them. I'd love to see Marsali again." She inhaled. "Tide's coming in," she said, watching a wave roll over the dry sand higher on the beach. "I suppose I should get back and help Dad with dinner. If he'll let me, that is."

"I'm sure he wouldn't mind help. He's let me pitch in a few times."

"Really?"

"Yeah. Why do you say it like that?" he asked, repeating her words from earlier.

The air left her lungs in a huff. "It's just…he doesn't usually let anyone help. The kitchen has always been his domain, even when my mom was alive."

"Maybe he thought chopping all of those veggies might help my dexterity," he said, flexing the hand of the injured left arm.

"No sling?"

"Not at the moment."

Which meant what? "Going against doctor's orders?"

"Not exactly."

Uh-huh. "You know—"

"It's hard to run while wearing a sling," he said. "And it's nearing the end of the time required to wear it. Now can I ask you a question?"

"You rescued me from death by sinking sand, so sure. Ask away."

"What's the deal with you and the garage apartment? I mean, I'd think staying in the house would be the norm when a kid comes home to visit her parents."

"Oh, that. Yeah, you'd think." She inhaled and exhaled in a rush, wishing the salty breeze would carry away her frustration. She'd known dealing with her dad wouldn't be easy, but she'd hoped it wouldn't be as strained as it was.

"If it's too personal, you don't have to answer."

"No, it's fine. I'm sure you noticed the tension between me and my dad."

"Some."

"Yeah…well, my dad and I haven't gotten along in a lot of years because he didn't want me to marry Tommy's father. When I did, well, that was that. In his words, he washed his hands of me."

"Ouch. Tough to hear but you can't believe things said in anger."

"Maybe," she mused. "But then," she said, giving the words a dramatic flair she didn't feel, "I had Tommy and we brought him to meet his grandparents for the first time. I thought we'd be in the house, too. In my old room, where I was today. Instead my poor Mom met us at the car with tears in her eyes and told Scott to take our bags up to the garage. In anticipation of our visit, my dad had finished the upstairs of the garage. We've stayed there every trip since."

It was an embarrassing story to tell because her father had literally finished the apartment to keep her and Scott from sleeping under the same roof as him. But the story was hers all the same.

"I see. Will your husband be joining you? Should I try to find another place to stay?"

A slow huff left her and she shifted her gaze to the water. "No. No, there's no need for that. Scott was… He was KIA. Baghdad."

"I'm sorry to hear that."

"Thanks. Dad didn't like Scott, although I don't think he would've approved of *any*one at that stage of my life, but when I told them I was getting married at seventeen and that I was pregnant, Dad lost it. Did the whole *I forbid you* thing. So, the eve of my eighteenth birthday, Scott helped me sneak out of my room, and we ran away to get married."

"Wow. I bet that went over well with Tom."

She turned toward the stairs leading over the dunes, and they silently fell into step beside each other. "About how you'd think, especially since we were banished to the apartment afterwards. I suppose it was a bit dramatic, but we knew we'd never get his permission, and we couldn't wait. Didn't want to wait, especially since Scott was already through basic and about to be stationed. To get military housing, we had to be married so…"

"What happened then? After you snuck out and got married, I mean?"

A smile formed and she couldn't stop it. "We went on a week-long camping honeymoon in a state park since it was all we could afford. Yes, I am that woman who spent her honeymoon in a tent. But once the week was over, we went home to face my parents."

Her laugh belied the drama of the time. All she had to do was close her eyes and she could see the fury on her father's face. And the disappointment. "Yeah. There was a lot of yelling, then silence. And it's been tense ever since."

"That's a long time to hold a grudge, especially if you stayed together. Was it something specific Tom didn't like about your husband?"

"You mean other than getting his seventeen-year-old daughter pregnant?"

"I imagine most fathers would feel that way."

Maybe. But her pregnancy wasn't the worst of her father's upset. No, according to Tom Blanchette, Scott had no common sense.

Thirteen years later, she now understood why her father had felt that way at least from a financial standpoint. Still, one thing she knew not to do over the years was to ever say anything derogatory about Scott to her parents. Ever.

But somehow it seemed her dad had known the entire time. "I should get back. Enjoy your walk."

"Actually I'm headed that way myself. Do you mind if I walk with you?"

"Oh, uh, no. That's fine."

The climb up the stairs from the beach always left her winded after crossing the soft, shifting sand. When she made it to the top, she paused along the outcropping to spray her feet with one of the hoses and donned the flip-flops she carried.

"Ready?" he asked when she finished.

"Yeah," she said, turning to side-eye him when he placed a hand at the small of her back as a crowd of people approached. He placed himself a bit toward the middle of the walkway, forcing the group to go single file, and the gesture struck her as…protective?

Once in the clear, she glanced up at him and decided that maybe they'd gotten off on the wrong foot due to the apartment mess. "I'm sorry for what I said today. About your job. What you do is important, obviously," she said, lifting her hand to indicate his injury.

"It's just not for you."

"I'm not a factor in the equation," she said, feeling his gaze on her face. "But no. Every time Scott deployed, I had insomnia until he came home."

"You know, you could just as easily get killed in a car accident."

"I suppose that's true. But that doesn't change the extremely high level of danger some professions have."

"Meaning mine."

"If it fits."

"So you're saying if I wasn't a bodyguard, you'd date me?"

Chapter 7

Denz watched the shocked expression flash over Claire's face and cringed. But learning she was single had upped his interest in the beautiful woman beside him, and he didn't like that something like a job—one he was good at—might keep him from getting to know her a little better.

"Hypothetically, you mean?" she asked.

"Yeah," he said. "Sure. The subject came up earlier with Mrs. B and now…I'm curious."

"Why did it come up?"

"She offered to set me up while I'm here."

"To match you?"

"Yeah."

"I see," she murmured. "Well, my answer would be no."

He fell into step beside her as they made their way down the sidewalk away from the pier, toward the streets and houses beyond, and moved to her right side so that he was on the outside, closest to the road and any approaching danger. "Because of my job."

"That's one of the reasons."

Having known him a matter of hours, how many had she come up with? "Have you dated since your husband died?"

Claire flashed him another look with her wary eyes and shook her head.

"It's only been a year," she said, sounding somewhat defensive, "and Tommy… He's having trouble adjusting. Dating is the last thing I need to be doing right now."

"I'm not so sure about that."

"What do you mean?"

"I don't know, it's just maybe what he needs is to see his mother living her life again."

"I live."

"He may also need a man's presence since that's what he's missing—his father."

The light changed and they had to pause at a cross-walk. He noted Claire's silence and the quiet concentration on her face as she pondered his words.

"I'd hoped some time with my dad might help Tommy sort some things out. That he'd open up and talk."

Denz knew he was getting too personal, but he couldn't seem to stop the curiosity riding him where she was concerned. "What about you?"

"What do you mean?"

What *did* he mean? "I'm just wondering if coming here isn't a first step toward whatever's next for you. If you're hoping to find something here?"

Claire glanced up at him and then quickly away.

"I'm not sure yet." She was silent a long moment. Then, "Are you close to your father?"

The question was simple in its essence but held the weight of time and distance and far too little communication. "No. I mean, there aren't any issues between us, but I wouldn't say we're close."

The light changed and the walk signal flashed. They stepped off into the street in unison and continued away from the pier.

"Why not?" she asked.

Denz knew ducking the question wasn't possible. "It's nothing big or dramatic. My dad was career military and away a lot. By the time he retired, I'd enlisted and our paths crossed at the door."

"That's…sad."

"Why? I had a great childhood. I grew up on bases with lots of other kids like me. We all knew the score."

"Yeah, but you just said you don't know your father," she murmured.

"Did Tommy know his father well?"

Her mouth pinched at the question and Denz got the feeling he'd struck a nerve.

"Where are they now? Your parents?" she asked.

"My dad lives on the outskirts of Savannah, and my mom passed away when I was still in the military."

"Oh, I'm sorry to hear that."

"Thanks. She was a great mom, always did her best even though with her health she never felt all that great."

The noise around the pier lessened as they made their way down the quiet streets. Every so often, Claire's wet feet squeaked against her flip-flops.

The quiet was one of the things he'd liked about Carolina Cove when he'd been assigned here to guard Oliver and Marsali last spring and fall.

The small beach town could be tourist crazy during the season, but he knew from the time he'd spent here that, once the season was over, it was peaceful. Much like the side streets they now walked.

"Have you seen your dad since the shooting? Did he come to the hospital?"

"Nah. It wasn't life-threatening."

"I'd think getting shot at all would constitute a threat," she countered.

"He gets contacted if I'm ever critical." He'd taken two steps before he realized she'd stopped walking. "Something wrong?"

She raised her eyebrows and stared up at him, looking adorable with her face scrunched up to combat the setting sun.

"He's notified if you're *critical?* Are you saying he doesn't even know you got shot?"

Denz inhaled, befuddled by her upset. "I haven't told him."

"And you don't think he has a right to know? He's your *father.*"

"Do you tell your father everything?" The question hit home given her expression, and the niggle of suspicion regarding her motives for being there turned into a full-fledged punch. "Ah. I thought so. You're *not* just here for a vacation, are you?"

She put her feet into motion and nudged by him on the narrow sidewalk.

"Of course I am."

"Doesn't ring true, sweetheart."

She stopped again, and because he'd been following her marching steps so closely, he nearly ran into her. Claire tilted her head back, way back, and stared up at him.

"I'm not your sweetheart."

"Just making conversation as we walk."

"Making conversation? I don't know you and you're asking a lot of personal questions."

"So are you."

"For all I know, that story about you being a bodyguard is a lie, and when my dad checked you out, he talked to a friend of yours who covered for you. People do that kind of stuff all the time."

Denz chuckled, his laughter echoing off of the homes nearby.

"It's not funny."

"It's a little funny. Especially considering who I had dinner with tonight."

"Who you *claim* to have had dinner with."

"Claire," he said, gently snagging her arm with his one good hand, "I'm legit. I'm not sure who your father talked to, but I can provide credentials if you'd like to see them. Or I could prove it to you another way."

"What do you mean?" she asked.

"I need a date for a wedding."

Claire blinked.

"A wedding—with Oliver Beck and Marsali in attendance?"

Yeah, he really didn't like the fact the draw for her was Oliver. "They'll be there," he said. "But since you know Marsali, and she can vouch for me, maybe you'll finally believe I am who I say I am. Plus Mrs. B can help you with your dating issue."

"I don't have a dating issue."

"Good. That means you'll go with me. Because a wedding date isn't really a date but an event, and you're only going to make sure I am who I say I am."

He could practically see the wheels spinning in her brain as she pondered his words.

Claire inhaled and moved forward without responding to his question as to whether or not she'd go with him. Denz followed, trying not to notice the sway of her hips or how cute she looked as she squeak-flopped along the sidewalk.

"Marsali set Scott and me up," she said. "In high school."

Okay. Not sure he wanted to hear that but…

"If I agree to go," she said, the words trailing over her shoulder, "it definitely wouldn't be as a date—because I don't. But *if* I agreed, whose wedding is it? *Where* is it?"

He chuckled at her attempt to fish for details. "Uh-uh. You want info, you have to agree first."

"Seriously?" She stopped again and turned to face him, inhaling as though drawing on the last of her patience. "Fine, I'll go—only so I can see them together in person and say hello to Marsali."

"Of course."

"Okay. I agree. So who's getting married?"

Chapter 8

The following morning, Claire knocked on Tommy's bedroom door before letting herself inside. Her son was still asleep, looking adorably rumpled and much too old given the way his long, lanky form sprawled both on and off the twin bed.

She shook her head at the clothes he hadn't put away and set about quietly straightening the room. Her father had always been particular about the house, though she'd noticed things had lapsed a bit since her mother had passed.

She gathered Tommy's slides and set them toward the end of the bed when she spotted a cord sticking out from under the coverlet.

Blood pressure rising, she gently tugged and, sure enough, the game system that was supposedly secure in her bedroom closet *wasn't*. "Oh, no, you didn't. Tommy? Tommy, wake up."

She got to her feet and jostled his shoulder, getting a nasty four-letter response from him. "*Excuse* me? You did not just use that kind of language with me."

"Mom?"

"Yes, Mom. Wake up. Now."

"Why?" he asked with a groan while pulling the pillow over his head. "I thought we're on vacation?"

"I can't believe you. One day? You couldn't behave for *one* day?"

"What are you—"

He rolled over in time to see her bend and pull the bag from beneath his bed, and his eyes widened. Claire shook her head back and forth. "You bought yourself another month."

"No!"

"Yes. *Three* suspensions, bad grades, and now this? Tommy, what are you thinking?" she asked as she turned.

Tommy grabbed her so fast Claire didn't know what happened. One minute she was walking away from the bed and the next she tumbled backward, gasping from the pain of his grip on her arms as he toppled her to the bed and scrambled over her.

"It's mine!"

"Tommy!"

The wrestling match lasted mere seconds but seemed like hours, her son stronger as he tightened his grip until she was forced to let go. He rolled off the bed, kneeing her in the process, and took off out the door in only his boxers.

"What's going on in there?" her father asked from the hallway.

Claire quickly wiped the pained tears from her eyes and got to her feet so that, by the time her father entered the room, she was bent over the bed, making it up.

"Claire?"

"Sorry, Dad, did we wake you?"

"You'd wake the dead with all the racket you two were making. What happened?"

She had to sniffle and swallow the lump in her throat. "Uh, Tommy. He got excited b-because I let him have his game system back earlier than expected."

"Well, where'd he go with it?"

"I'm not sure. I'll ask when he gets back." Claire felt her father's gaze boring a hole into her as she fussed over the bed, but he eventually seemed satisfied with her answers and left.

Seconds later, she heard him in the kitchen filling the coffeepot. Her weak knees folded as she sat on the edge of the taut covers and wrapped her arms around her waist to hug.

What on earth had just happened?

She and Tommy had gotten into arguments plenty of times, but he'd never laid his hands on—

"Coffee's on."

"O-okay, thanks!" she called, taking a breath and forcing herself to her feet.

She fixed the bed once more and hurried down the hall toward her bedroom, locking herself inside. She needed a long shower and some time to think before she faced her father again.

Not to mention her son.

DENZ WAS SITTING on the steps leading up to the apartment with his coffee and a real estate guide he'd picked up at the gas station that morning when he spotted Claire's son tearing out of the house like it was on fire.

He started to stand and go see what was up, but the kid stopped near his mom's Jeep and started crying. Sobs racked the kid's shoulders, and he hid behind the vehicle, obviously not wanting to be seen.

Remembering his own reaction at that age to people seeing him lose his cool, Denz stayed silent and still and hoped the kid wouldn't notice him.

After a few minutes, the kid pulled himself together and took off around the garage, still carrying whatever it was he'd run out of the house with.

Denz used the opportunity to quietly go inside, taking a few discreet glances out of the windows around the apartment. He finally spotted the kid placing the game system bag inside one of Tom's outside storage boxes. The kid's head jerked all around as though to see if he was being watched while he worked to cover it up and close the lid.

When the kid skulked away, Denz tracked him from within the apartment once more. Tommy stood outside the back of the house long seconds before heading inside as quickly as he'd emerged.

Interesting happenings this morning, he mused.

All of which reminded him of his talk with Claire about her relationship with her father. Something had picked at him ever since, and he inhaled and pulled out his cell, scrolling through his contacts until he found the right one.

He stared at the name, at the number, his thumb hovering over the digits. Another inhalation had him swiping the contact list away and shoving his phone back in his pocket.

It was early yet. Too early to call.

And definitely too early for whatever had just taken place to send Claire's son tearing outside in his underwear and tears.

Back in the kitchenette area, he dumped the last of his coffee in the sink, gazing out the window toward the house once more.

It was Saturday morning in a beach town with summer kicking in. Time to go find some sand.

He changed into swim trunks and grabbed the towel he'd picked up at one of the tourist traps last week.

Tom had told him to borrow whatever he needed from the supplies below, so once he had sunscreen, earbuds, and a small cooler filled, he tossed a book into the backpack with the towel and other items and headed out to find a chair.

While wandering around the garage, he relocated the bag carrying the game system to his vehicle and locked up it up until he got the full story.

That done, he rounded the rental, found a chair, and went back to the steps to retrieve the backpack he'd left there. That's when he saw Claire standing on the porch. "Morning."

"Good morning."

Okay. Yeah, something was definitely off. One glance told him Tommy wasn't the only one in tears that morning. "You okay?" he asked, moving toward her.

"What? Oh, I'm fine."

He wondered how long it would take her to realize simply standing outside looking like a kicked puppy was a little telling. "Lose something?" he asked instead.

Her gaze met his, eyes wide.

"I saw him stash it. It's now locked in my car. Do you want me to get it for you?"

"No. No, if you don't mind, just leave it."

"Okay."

"You're off to the beach. Looks like it's going to be a beautiful day."

It would've been if he wasn't so focused on the fact her eyes were puffy, she sounded congested from her tears, and he could tell by the tone of her voice that she was more than a little upset. "Why don't you come with me?"

"What?"

"Just for a little while."

"Oh, I shouldn't. I need to do some things and—"

"Come on. It's Saturday and, if I'm not mistaken, the first day of your vacation?"

"It…is."

"Well, first days of vacation should be spent doing something fun. Let's go hit the sand, breathe in the salt air, and forget our troubles for an hour or two. What do you say?"

Chapter 9

Claire hadn't intended to say yes, but somehow she'd found herself back in the house, changing into a swimsuit, and glaring at Tommy's door as she'd walked by.

She hadn't bothered knocking when she'd opened the door, but she'd noted he was back in bed, his head on the pillow as though he hadn't a care in the world.

She supposed she ought to be thankful he'd returned so soon after running out of the house like that, but she felt it had more to do with his state of undress than the fact he'd wanted to revisit their situation and discuss what he'd done.

She'd been in her room when she'd heard his familiar stride in the hall and winced when his door had closed just shy of a slam.

Knowing Tommy couldn't have taken the system far, she'd gone out to take a look at possible hiding places when Denz had spotted her.

A grackle squawked overhead, drawing her out of her dazed state to the beach in front of her now.

"Claire? You sure you're okay?" Denz asked.

Claire turned her head and tried not to notice how good Denz looked in his swim trunks. The man's shoulder was still scarred and bruised, but he had a good tan and plenty of muscles, and even staring at her from behind his dark aviators, he looked, well, *good*. "Just a lot on my mind."

"I've been told I'm a good listener."

Oh, she was sure he'd been told a lot of things. But how could she share what had happened with Tommy when her brain had yet to process it? Who was that angry, bitter boy who'd made her gasp and cry with pain? "Tommy and I had a fight."

"I gathered as much. Anything I can do to help?"

She and Denz had sat there in silence for the last thirty minutes or so, staring at the ocean while breathing in the salt air. Now she grabbed her sunscreen and debated on whether or not to ask her next question. "No. Um, I need to turn. Would you…mind?" she asked, holding up the spray. "Just my back."

"No problem."

She watched as he shoved himself up out of the beach chair and took the two steps toward hers. He extended a hand, and she automatically accepted it, only to regret it when she saw his head tilt and his mouth firm.

Claire quickly shoved the spray at him and pulled her hand away, forcing him to hurry to catch it.

She turned and gave him her back, pulling her braided hair over her shoulder to give him full access.

Her modest suit would definitely be considered a "mom" suit in that it was a one-piece with full coverage, but both sides of the black suit were split, with thin, black straps crisscrossing both sides from breast to hip. She'd liked the little detail when she'd purchased it because it gave the otherwise plain suit some interest, but now even that felt like too much when she was so aware of Denz's gaze.

The spray was cold as he moved it over her back, but it was the shock of his large hand rubbing the sunscreen in that rocked her. She hadn't expected that, and even though he only touched her upper shoulders and neck, she found herself sucking in air to combat the alluring desire to lean back, just for a moment, and let someone else hold her upright.

What she wouldn't give for someone to lean on right now. A partner. A friend. Someone to share the load she carried.

"That should do it," he murmured, his voice low and husky near her ear. "Unless you want me to spray your legs."

"N-no, I've got it. Thanks."

"My turn?"

Realizing she'd fallen into a trap of her own making, she forced a smile and turned. "Of course."

Denz moved to his chair and retrieved the bottle of sunscreen he'd used earlier when they'd arrived.

She tossed the spray into her bag, only then realizing his sunscreen was lotion and that meant… Okay.

He handed off the bottle and turned, and she forced herself to focus on squeezing the lotion into her hand rather than on the broad expanse of his muscled back.

The first touch was the hardest, but she bit her lip and smeared the lotion with quick, efficient motions. Because he had a lot more skin exposed, it took a bit longer to perform the favor, and by the time she finished, she'd eaten off the lip balm she'd applied earlier. "O-okay, done."

He turned to face her and held out a hand for the lotion. She complied and realized her mistake when his large hand closed over hers and held. She knew with certainty that he saw the finger bruises beginning to darken and pulled away to make a show of carefully spreading her towel on the sand.

"Uh, you forgot something."

Just about to drop to her knees to hide from the look she knew she received from behind those sunglasses, she turned. "What?"

Denz grabbed her spray from atop the bag where she'd dropped it and gently grasped her elbow, lifting it slightly to spray the crisscrosses and exposed skin on her sides. First one, then the other. "Oh, yeah. Th-thanks."

"Yup," he said softly.

He didn't move away, and Claire got the feeling he wanted to say something but wasn't sure how. She quickly turned and dropped to her towel, ending the possibility that he might mention the bruises.

They sunbathed in silence, and after a bit, she was able to take a breath and settle into the welcoming sand. Her lashes grew heavy despite her rampant thoughts and worries, and she found herself dozing off and waking up as people walked by to find their spot for the day or the birds squawked nearby.

"Claire? Hey, Claire…"

She opened her eyes and spotted a hairy kneecap in her line of vision. That was followed by a strong thigh and the navy blue of Denz's trunks. "Oh," she said, rising to her elbows. "I fell asleep."

"You did. I hate to wake you but you're going to burn. Time to turn or pack up for the day."

"Turn. I don't want to leave yet." Because if she left, she had to go back to the house and confront Tommy, and right now, she just didn't have the words or the brain power to form them.

"Your call," Denz said, getting to his feet. "I'm going for a swim to cool down. You wanna come?"

She squinted up at him, amazed by the sense of security she felt in his presence despite the fact she'd only known him a day. Denz had that solid presence about him, though.

Maybe it was because of what had happened with Tommy, but whatever it was, for the moment, she decided she liked it. "First day of vacation, right? Why not?"

After another hour at the beach, they decided it best to leave. The sand was getting crowded, the sun hotter, and despite sunscreen, they both looked a little pink.

They packed up and headed toward the bridge leading over the dunes, and Claire was thankful she'd taken the time to separate herself from what had happened with her son. Time to cool down and look at it from a less emotional perspective.

Tommy was obviously having difficulties adjusting to his father's death, and anger emerged because of it. Acting out in school, the attitude.

Tommy had gone to counseling provided by the military for a time but then said he didn't want to go, and she hadn't pushed it. Now she wished she had.

"I realize I'm a stranger to you," Denz murmured as they left the hoses and water behind and headed down the street toward the house. "But sometimes it's easier to talk to a stranger than someone you know."

Her steps faltered, but after a slight stumble, she kept going. "I'm fine."

It was a mantra she'd repeated every day for the last year. Actually, longer. One that often came to her lips when she felt overwhelmed by responsibilities and life and her husband was overseas and not at her side to deal with the financial stress he'd placed on them with his decisions.

"Just making the offer."

"Thanks."

"Claire—"

"I'm fine," she said again, picking up her pace. "It'll all be fine."

Because when it came down to it, what other option was there?

Chapter 10

Later that afternoon, Denz was outside with a battery-operated screwdriver, securing the stair treads leading up to the apartment. Tom had given him such a good rate on the weekly rental, Denz figured a few odd jobs here and there couldn't hurt.

A door slammed and Denz turned to find Tommy carrying a bag of trash.

He watched as the kid rounded the garage to where the cans were stored in back and then set the tool aside to follow.

The kid had tossed the trash into the can without properly securing the lid and had turned to head back when he realized Denz blocked the path. "Hey."

"Hey."

"Might want to fasten that down. It'll keep you from having to come clean it all up when the animals get into it at night."

Denz could tell Tommy didn't appreciate being corrected, but he secured the lid. That done, the kid tried to slide by Denz. "Hold up."

Tommy shot Denz a wary look.

"I may be wrong, and I hope to God that I am, but I want an answer. Did you put those bruises on your mother's arms?"

The kid paled to the color of snow, and Denz felt a rage roll through him unlike any he'd felt in a very long time. He grabbed the kid by his shirt and shoved him back against the garage, meeting Tommy eye to eye. "You hurt your *mother*?"

"It was an accident. I got mad."

"There is no excuse for it. *None*," he growled into the kid's face. "And if I ever find out you've touched her like that again, I don't care if I'm on the other side of the world, I *will* come find you and show you what it's like to be hurt by someone our size. Do you understand me?"

"Y-yes."

"I mean it, kid. There won't be a rock you can climb under to hide from me if you ever touch her that way again."

"I won't but—"

"Oh, no. No buts," Denz said with another shove against the garage.

"Why do you care so much?"

"Seriously? Because I'm a man and what you did to her is the trademark of scum. And just so we're clear—that bag you stashed is now in my possession, so don't be bothering your mother about it."

"That's *mine*."

"Finders keepers," Denz said grimly.

"Is there a problem here?" Tom asked from the corner of the garage.

Denz held Tommy's gaze and watched the kid's eyes widen even bigger than before. Yeah, the kid knew he'd be in even deeper if Grandpa found out.

Denz stepped back and released Tommy's shirt, never taking his gaze off the kid. "No. Not anymore."

"Tommy?"

"No, sir."

Tommy slid along the wall of the garage and headed toward his grandfather, head ducked.

"Tommy, my truck needs washed. Get to it," Tom ordered.

"I was going to the beach."

"Well, now you're washing my truck," Tom ordered gruffly. "You can go after. *If* your mother says it's okay."

The kid hesitated for a second, red-faced, but then left them with a final glare at Denz.

"Do I want to know what that was about?" Tom asked.

"No, sir, you don't."

"You'll let me know if something changes and I do?"

Denz nodded.

Tom seemed satisfied with Denz's response and carried the second, smaller bag of trash toward the can.

"Thanks for fixing up those stairs."

"No problem."

"Thank you for that, too," Tom added. "That boy has an awful big chip he's carrying around, and whatever caused you to set him straight must have been a doozy."

Denz didn't speak. He planned to keep a close watch on both Tommy and Claire while he was in town, but if there was a need to involve Claire's father, he would. He couldn't stand the thought of her trying to take on Tommy's anger alone.

"So, I hear you're going to a wedding?"

CLAIRE FINISHED her post-beach shower and donned a pair of cutoff shorts and a tank top. Given that it was Saturday and the first day of their stay, as Denz had pointed out, she gave herself the day off to regroup from the last couple of years—and this morning.

She found a lightweight, long-sleeved top she'd brought with her for breezy evenings on the beach. Claire tied it at her waist, then rolled the sleeves at the cuff, careful of the length so that they covered the bruises.

She'd avoided Tommy since her return, but when she went in search of him to have that talk, she discovered him washing her father's truck. "Okay," she murmured, wondering how that had come about when she hadn't been able to get him to do any such chores for ages. Not since before Scott's death.

"He's not doing too bad a job," her father said from behind her.

"Hey, Dad. I thought you were going in to work?"

"I got someone to cover. There's a music event downtown but nothing my guy can't handle. Thought I'd stick around."

Awkward silence filled the space between them, and she shifted against the countertop where she leaned. "I, um, thought I'd make some sandwiches for lunch. Something simple. Sound good?"

"I can do that."

"I'd like to help. I know you're not used to having Tommy and me here—"

"That's not my doing."

"I didn't say it was, Dad, I just meant—" She broke off and took a breath, determined to not be drawn into butting heads with him as she always was. "If you want to make them, great. If you want help, let me know."

"I've gotten along okay since your mother passed," he

said, moving to the fridge.

Claire leaned her weight against the counter behind her and tracked her father's movements. "I know. I'm sorry. Actually, Dad, I'd like to talk about that. Apologize for not being here to help more."

"You had a husband and son and a job. Didn't expect you to."

"I know you didn't *expect* it, but I wish… Dad, I just wish things were different between us. That's all."

"Things are fine."

Oh, how familiar *that* sounded. "Look, Dad—"

"You need to keep an eye on your boy."

She didn't like the sound of that. "Why do you say that?"

"Denz had a chat with Tommy earlier."

Claire cringed, the statement confirming her earlier fears that Denz had indeed noticed the bruises forming and had guessed as to the origin. "Do you, uh, know what it was about?"

"Denz wouldn't say. But if you want my advice, you need to get the boy in hand now before it's too late. He's got a lot of growing and learning to do still, and if a man like Denz is pinning the boy against the wall, Tommy's in for a world of trouble."

Pinning him against the wall? "I'll take care of it." Oh, would she ever take care of it. No one was going to lay a finger on her son without suffering the consequences.

"Denz has been working ever since you two got back from the beach. You want to help?" her father asked. "Go ask him what he wants on his sandwich. If he's going to play handyman, the least I can do is feed him."

She grabbed on to the excuse with both hands and headed for the door, anger fueling her steps. "My pleasure."

Chapter 11

Claire stalked by Tommy without comment and continued on. Denz was nowhere in sight. No longer working on the stairs, nor searching for tools in the garage beneath.

She took a fortifying breath and eyed the apartment door before jogging up the treads, too angry to appreciate the fact they no longer shook.

The door opened just as she reached the top and she pushed her way inside.

"Uh, come in."

"Close the door."

A soft click sounded behind her.

Claire stalked across the small living area, her anger making her entire body tremble. "Did you put your hands on my son?"

"Claire—"

"Answer me."

"You already know I did or you wouldn't be asking the question," he said, leaning back against the wooden panel and crossing his arms over his chest.

"How dare you? What right do you have to touch him? You're a grown man!"

"Why are you wearing long sleeves?"

"What?"

"It's eighty-five outside and you're in long sleeves. How come?"

"We are discussing you bullying a thirteen-year-old child, not my wardrobe."

"That *child* is the size of a grown man, and he wasn't afraid to use his strength or his anger against his own mother."

Blasted by truth, she turned away from him and stalked as far as she was able before whirling around again. "What did you say to him? What did you do?"

Denz lowered his arms and walked toward the couch. "I made it clear he'd better not do it again."

Claire watched as he donned the sling, wincing as he fit the strap over his head. "You're never going to heal if you keep hurting yourself and working like that."

A small smile stole over his handsome face and he met her gaze.

"I thought you were angry with me."

"I *am*. You have no right—"

"I do, actually."

"How on earth do you figure that?"

"Claire, I have a job because kids like that grow up to be men who can't control their anger. They hurt the people around them, or they stalk someone because they can't handle reality. All of those raging hormones and all of that anger need to be channeled into something fast, before Tommy self-destructs."

She deflated at his words, knowing it was true. "I don't... He's different now. He wasn't like that before his dad… I'm not sure how to handle it," she said softly. "But he's never done that before. He's never hurt me."

"Maybe not. But now that he has, the next time won't be as big a deal."

"It was a one-time thing. I'm sure of it."

Oh, the way Denz stared at her. The look he gave her.

"Are you? Because it's not just you we're talking about here. It could be a future girlfriend or a violent incident at his school."

No. "Stop. Please. Tommy's not going to hurt anyone."

"He already did—you."

She sank onto the arm of the couch, legs weak.

"Claire—"

She got up and turned away again, moving toward the window to stare down at Tommy below. "Before Scott died, Tommy was a straight-A student who never got into trouble. This year? He barely passed and was suspended *three* times. He's fallen into the wrong group of friends, won't do what he's told. That's why we had to cancel our visit a few weeks ago. He had to serve his punishment."

"So that's why you're here," he said softly. "It's not for a simple visit or vacation."

She closed her eyes, shook her head.

"I can talk to him."

She glanced at Denz and frowned. "Like you did earlier?"

"If that's what it takes. Look, Claire, you can't let this continue. You have to set him straight now."

"You sound like my father."

"Does Tom know any of this?"

"Only that Tommy is struggling. N-nothing else. Dad told me that if you had to take Tommy to task, something big must have happened and I needed to do something."

"You know he's right."

"Telling Dad about Tommy getting suspended is one thing, but I can't tell Dad that Tommy..." She lifted her arm slightly to indicate the bruises.

"Your father might surprise you."

"Maybe. Or he could get rougher with Tommy than you did, and that's not something I'm okay with."

"You don't want them fighting. I get it. Tom knows I handled something, though. And that I'll do it again if needed."

If needed? "I'll talk to Tommy. I-I just... I don't know what to do," she said softly, the words bitter in their truth. "I ground Tommy and he sneaks out. I drop him off at school and watch him go in the front door only to get a call later that he's skipped because he's walked out after I left. He's completely and totally obsessed with that game system. It holds the most leverage, but when I take that away, he freaks out."

"That was the cause of the fight this morning?"

"Yeah. I went to wake him up and discovered that he'd stolen the system out of my room. When I told him he'd lost it for another month, he...grabbed me. We fought and he took it."

"Have you talked to him since this morning?"

She shook her head and blinked at the sting of tears. "I haven't. I'm not sure how or what to say. I mean...what do you say?"

"It has to be addressed, Claire. That's violence. Abuse."

"I *know*. It's just... I have to figure out the best approach. One that isn't physical," she added, pursing her lips.

"I think I got my point across."

He stated it with a twinkle in his eyes and she found herself shaking her head. "I suppose instead of yelling at you I should be thanking you. If Dad hadn't said— Oh! Lunch. I totally forgot. Dad's making sandwiches and wanted to know what you like on yours."

"Anything's fine," he said. "I'm not picky. Claire, are you going to be okay?"

The question gave her pause, but only because she wasn't sure of the answer. "I'll be fine. We'll be fine."

Denz lifted his good hand and tapped his injured shoulder.

"Might be a little messed up but it's here if you need it."

Sweet. That was all she could think as she stared at the handsome man across from her and the air left her lungs. Today on the beach, she'd wanted so badly for someone to lean on and shoulder the burden and responsibilities, and here Denz was volunteering.

He'd taken a bold step where her son was concerned, but after talking with him, she realized it was out of fear for her and who Tommy could become if he continued on the way that he was. She reminded herself Denz was the type of man who ran into the burning building, not away. And he'd done just that with Tommy. "Thank you."

"You're welcome."

"I-I should go. Come and eat when you're ready."

"Yeah. Okay."

He moved to the door and opened it for her, and she felt small and feminine as she walked by him. She'd always been attracted to tall guys, but Scott had been lean whereas Denz was more solidly built.

"Claire?"

She paused on the landing and turned, her teeth sinking into her lower lip as she waited for whatever he was about to say.

"You're a good mom. Don't let this thing with Tommy make you think differently."

"How do you know what kind of mom I am?" she asked, reminding herself as well as him that it had been a whole twenty-four hours since they'd met. Granted, a lot had happened in those hours, but still. She couldn't let a handsome face and kind offer change her perspective when it came to his job—or his interest, if he even was interested in her.

"Sweetheart, you were fit to be tied when I opened this door, ready to defend your baby boy. That's what a good mom does. What she doesn't do is back down. Understand?"

Chapter 12

Claire waited until that evening to approach Tommy. Her father had left the house to take his evening walk, so she used the opportunity for what it was. "Turn off the television."

Tommy's face turned red and his mouth immediately set into a hard line, but he did as he was told. Small victory that was. "Do you have anything to say for yourself?"

The words were softly spoken but firm, and she watched her son simply shrug. "Really? Nothing?"

"It's my game."

The air left her lungs in a loud *ha* that left Tommy flinching. "Your game. Who paid for it?"

"You," he said begrudgingly.

"And who got it taken away because of his behavior and, I might add, *illegal* actions?"

No response once more. She shook her head, her entire body trembling from the force of her emotions. From the upset and anger and frustration of not being able to break through the shell he'd built around himself in the last year. "Tommy—"

"I'm sorry. Happy now? I didn't mean to— I just didn't want you to take my game."

"So you *hurt* me?" She yanked up one sleeve and moved toward him. "Look. *Look!*" she said again when he avoided doing what he was told.

The bruises had really formed now, dark and ugly against her skin. "Is *this* who you want to be? Someone you're proud of?"

She thought she saw the glistening of tears in his eyes and steeled herself against the way the sight made her mother's heart soften. "Are these the actions of someone your father would be proud of?"

"No! I'm sorry. I just got mad."

"And I got hurt because of it and that is *not* acceptable. We are responsible for our actions and reactions, no matter how angry we get."

"I know."

"Do you?"

"I just wanted my *game*."

"And you would have had it soon had you not behaved the way that you did. Actions have consequences, Tommy, and sneaking into my room and taking it when you know—"

"I just wanted to talk to them!" he shouted, hands fisted.

Talk to them? "What?"

Another lift and shrug of his bony shoulder.

"Oh, no. We are discussing this with words and you are going to use them. Talk to whom?"

A tear rolled down his cheek and he swiped a fist over his face.

"The guys."

"What guys? Kids from school?"

He shook his head and then—

"No. The… The guys. Dad's guys. From his unit."

The news nearly took her to her knees. As it was, she had to swallow hard and hug her arms around her front just to stay on her feet. "You…play with them?"

He nodded.

"H-how long have you… I mean—"

"Always. Some of the guys knew Dad and I played together before so…when they can, we play now. I have to log on to see when they're there, though."

She closed her eyes and fought for the breath seizing in her lungs. "Tommy, you could've told me."

"I thought it would make you sad."

"What makes me sad is that you've been doing stuff you shouldn't and getting in trouble for it, when all you had to do is be honest. And the anger and getting into trouble?"

"I'm sorry. *Really*. They yelled at me for that, too. Said I had to stop. I didn't mean to hurt you, Mom. I was asleep and then you were yelling and I just… I'm sorry. I won't do it again."

"I'd like to believe that."

"It's true."

"Tommy, you are your father's son. You're tall and strong and handsome," she said, her voice breaking. "But with that physicality comes responsibilities, and that means not hurting those smaller and weaker than you."

"I know."

She squared her shoulders and forced her arms to her sides as she walked over to the couch to sit beside him. "What did Denz say to you earlier today?"

Once again, Tommy's face filled with color.

"That it better not happen again."

She imagined that was the mild version of what had transpired given what Denz and her father had told her, but she accepted Tommy's version at face value. "And you said?"

"That I understood and it wouldn't. He has the system now," Tommy said, his tone bleak. "He saw me hide it and he took it."

"Well, considering your penchant for sneaking into my closet, maybe it's best if Denz keeps it for now."

"But—"

"No, Tommy. I understand you're grieving for Dad. I am, too. Some part of us will always grieve no matter how much time passes, but grief has to be dealt with properly, and behaving the way you've been… That's not the right way. Those boys at school, the suspensions… I'm going to make some calls. See if I can't get you back into counseling."

"No. I don't want to go."

In that moment, she remembered Denz's words about how mamas don't back down, and she straightened her spine. "Too bad. You're struggling, whether you'll admit it or not. And as your mother, it's my responsibility to help you or else I'm not doing my job. Understand?"

He didn't agree, but he didn't protest, either. "Grandpa will be back soon. I thought maybe we could see if he'd take us for a golf cart ride, just to check things out since it's been awhile since we've been here."

"Does he know?"

The question was asked in a small, thready voice that carried the weight of the shame Tommy felt. It made her feel better, knowing that he at least seemed to grasp the gravity of what he'd done and was regretful. "I haven't told him. And I won't, unless you force me to."

She started to get up when he stretched out a hand and pushed her sleeve up a bit. She watched as he swallowed hard and his lower lip trembled when he saw the black bruises.

"I'm sorry, Mom."

"I'm glad. Now it's time to prove it by never touching someone like that again. Yeah?"

"Yeah."

"Okay, so watch TV until Grandpa gets back. I'm going to go sit on the porch swing."

Claire left the couch and Tommy and made her way through the quiet house to the back door. Just as she pushed open the storm door, she heard the television click on again.

She softly closed the door and leaned her forehead against her hand after it latched. The porch smelled a bit musty, and she knew it came from the heat and humidity and years of storms.

But right now, it smelled like home and safety and memories, and she struggled to battle the fear and uncertainty rising up inside of her when she thought of the future and Tommy and all they had yet to face.

This too shall pass.

It was something her mother had often said whenever worries abounded and problems became troublesome. *This too shall pass.*

Even if it passes like a kidney stone, Claire mused.

Chapter 13

During the next week, Denz shared a couple of meals with Claire's family in the evenings after work. He found himself looking forward to that time, sitting there at the table and talking about their day.

Claire and Tommy were pitching in with Tom's business and working a few hours every day on set in hopes of spotting a celebrity, and Denz teased her about her fascination.

Denz had quickly lost the rose-colored glasses he'd first worn after joining Guardian Group and being assigned to guard celebrities. He'd been responsible for a few—not all but a few—who were a lot more trouble than he felt they were worth.

But maybe he'd head to the location anyway? See what was happening there?

Denz left his PT appointment and celebrated the fact he could lose the sling for good when his cell buzzed. "Denz," he said after looking at the face and seeing Eliza's business listed.

"Hi, it's Eliza Hayes. I just wanted to double-check that you are planning to attend Mac and V's wedding?"

"Yes."

"And do you have a plus-one?"

"I do."

"Oooh, the woman you mentioned?" she asked.

"Yes. Claire Simmons."

"Hmm. Doesn't ring a bell. Oh, and nice going the other day when you kept changing the subject whenever Marsali tried to steer you back to dating."

Denz paused outside the SUV he'd rented for his stay. "Thanks. Do you and Marsali know everyone on the island?" he asked with some amusement.

"Pretty much. Hey, it's a fairly small town when you boil it down, and we grew up here. Did your date?"

"Yeah. And she knows Marsali."

"*Really*? Well, I should know her then."

"Her father is Tom Blanchette."

"Oh, my gosh, you mean it's *Clairey Blanchette*! I haven't seen her since high school!"

Denz held the phone away from his ear at Eliza's excited squeal.

"Wait until I tell Marsali. Does she know?"

"Uh, I don't think so since you just made the connection."

"Hang on, I'm putting you on speaker so I can text her right now. Oh, it'll be good to see Claire. Is she as pretty as ever?"

Denz unlocked the door and tossed his gym bag inside before he got in, leaving the door open to combat the growing heat of the day. "She is," he said, picturing Claire as she'd been this morning, sitting on the porch swing with her laptop and a concentrated frown on her delicate face as she'd worked on whatever it was on her screen.

"What's she doing these days?"

"She's at the location shoot with her father in craft service. I'm actually heading over there. Oliver gave me a pass to get by security."

"Ha! Like you'd need a pass. I bet you could get on past security if you set your mind to it, couldn't you?"

He smiled but didn't answer. Trade secrets were secrets, after all. "Want me to give Claire a message?"

"Yes, tell her we can't *wait* to see her."

"I'll be sure to tell her."

"Denz?"

"Yeah?"

"That comment you made at dinner about your relationships being brief?"

"What about it?"

"Claire's sweet. Be nice, okay?"

"I hear you."

"She lost her husband."

"I am aware."

"Are you…dating?"

"No," he said. "She's coming to confirm I'm actually a bodyguard."

"What?" Eliza asked, laughing.

Denz related the story with a sheepish grin and a shake of his head. "I think she's more interested in potentially rubbing shoulders with a certain celebrity we know."

"Ah," Eliza said, a smile in her voice. "Clairey always did follow that sort of thing. We all did in high school because we thought it was so cool that Marsali actually knew Oliver as he made his rise to stardom. Okay, well, I've got you both down and I can't wait to see you. And if Claire has any questions or wants to chat beforehand, please give her my number?"

"I'll do that. I think she could use a few friends right now."

"Oh?"

The moment the words left his mouth, he wished he could take them back.

"What's going on?" Eliza asked.

"I'll pass along your number, okay? I've got to get going or I'll hit the lunch traffic."

He heard her disgruntled sigh through the phone.

"Fine. But have her call me."

Denz tucked the phone away and finally closed the door of the rental, making the turn to head out to Ft. Fisher and the end of the island. Today's shoot was a series of beach scenes that were scheduled to last most of the day.

He parked and made the long walk toward the barricades, flashing the credentials Oliver had been kind enough to provide. Security let him through, and Denz made his way behind the area where cameras, tents, and all sorts of equipment had been set up.

While everyone watched the goings-on, Denz searched the crowd for any sign of the woman who'd been on his mind a lot the last week. Maybe it was because of the mama bear way she'd come to take him on in protection of her son or the quiet sadness and worry he saw in her sky-blue eyes, but whatever it was, he'd become uncomfortably aware he felt as hooked as the shark Tom had helped him land that fateful day.

He finally spotted what looked to be the craft service area and headed that way. His suspicions were confirmed when he saw Tommy lugging a bucket of ice in the same direction up ahead of him.

The kid's growing muscles bulged and reminded him of the idea he'd had today while doing his PT at one of

Mac's many investments—the gym. A tired kid had less anger, after all. And if a few hours a day and some proper training got the kid into something productive, all the better.

Denz followed Tommy toward the van and noted the open windows on either side. Inside were Tom, Claire, a young girl Denz didn't recognize, and another man who looked to be in his forties. Tommy joined them. "Starting to look like a clown car in there," he teased. "Think you can fit in a few more?"

"You volunteering?" Tom asked, grinning.

Denz shoved his sunglasses up on his head and felt it the moment Claire met his gaze. "I have a message for you."

She frowned. "Me?"

"Yeah. I confirmed you as my plus-one for the wedding and got a squeal of excitement from the wedding planner. You guys also went to high school together. Eliza Hayes, maiden name Bellefonte?"

"Oh, yeah. I remember her."

"She said to tell you she can't wait to see you," Denz said.

"You're going out?" Tommy asked. "Like a *date*?"

Realizing his mistake far too late, Denz cringed and met the kid's gaze. "Not exactly. Your mom agreed to accompany me to a wedding so I wouldn't have to go alone like a loser, that's all."

"No one likes to go to weddings alone," Claire told her son. "And"—she lowered her voice—"I might be able to meet Oliver Beck."

Someone called the scene via a bullhorn and people slowly began streaming their way.

"Give me your number and I'll text you her info," Denz said, ignoring Tom's fatherly stare.

Claire recited it while people began forming a line and placing orders, and Denz took a step back to give them room. "Okay, sent. Text me if you need anything."

Denz met Tom's gaze once more and nodded.

He lifted his hand and backed away, knowing he hadn't heard the last from his landlord when it came to his daughter.

Out of the crowd and over by the tents once more, he spotted Oliver talking to another member of Guardian Group. The man was built like a tank and stood out like a sore thumb, especially since he was dressed in slacks and a long-sleeved shirt, his gun in the shoulder strap he wore. Thankfully Bruce had removed the matching suit jacket considering it was an eighty-five-degree beach day.

Bruce spotted Denz and lifted his chin in greeting. Oliver turned and looked relieved.

"Oh, thank God. Perfect timing," Oliver said.

"What's going on?"

Oliver eyed Denz like a specimen under a microscope. "Something going on, Mr. Beck?"

Oliver ignored Denz's question and turned to look at the woman standing several feet away wearing a headset and hugging a clipboard to her chest.

"What do you think?" Oliver asked.

"Perfect height, size is off, but from a distance it won't matter. Looks are a great match, though," she said. "Yeah, he works."

"And the female lead?" Oliver asked.

"Now that we have him and we're down to the wire, I think I know the perfect one," the woman said. "I saw her earlier. Give me ten minutes. Twenty if she argues."

That said, the woman took off out of the tent and left Denz and Oliver alone. "What's going on?"

Denz glanced at Bruce and found the sweating man struggling to control his laughter.

"Our stars currently share a stomach bug." Oliver moved toward him and clapped a hand over Denz's shoulder. "Have you ever wondered what it would be like to be in *front* of the camera?"

"Can't say that I have," Denz said wryly.

"Well, let's try it and see what happens. Get him to wardrobe and makeup."

Shock rolled through him. "Uh, Mr. Beck, I'm not sure—"

"I am. Denz, you're about to be a hero of another sort."

Chapter 14

Everything happened so fast Claire wasn't sure what to make of it. One minute she'd been inside the van and the next some woman had yelped triumphantly and nearly shoved Tom out the pass-through in order to get to Claire.

"You. I have been looking everywhere for you. Come with me."

"Excuse me?"

"We need you and you're *perfect*. Come on," she said, grabbing Claire's hand. "Trust me, you'll be well compensated."

"I-I don't… Who are you?"

"We don't have time for that, hon."

"But—"

"Look, you want to make some easy money?"

Given her current life situation? "Depends on what I have to do."

The woman grinned. "Oh, honey, trust me, that won't be a problem."

"But—"

"You single?" the woman asked with barely suppressed impatience.

"Yes, why?"

"Perfect. Come on, we have to get you to makeup and wardrobe."

"My mom's going to be in the movie?" Tommy asked.

The woman stared up at Tommy and then looked at Claire's smaller frame. "Mom?"

"Yes," Claire said.

The woman sighed and rolled her eyes, her hand tightening on Claire's hand. "Some people get all the good genes. Let's go."

Thirty minutes later, Claire emerged from wardrobe in a chic black sleeveless dress with thigh-high slits up both sides. Oversized earrings completed the dazzling look, and someone handed her six-inch heels she thankfully didn't have to wear because they filmed on sand.

Her blond hair had been pulled into an elegant knot, with long tendrils framing her face, and her lips were coated with dark red lipstick that popped with her carefully lined eyes.

She didn't remember wearing this much makeup since her high school prom, but the artist assured her it was required due to the lighting and gist of the scene.

She carried the prop heels in her hand, and then the headset-wearing woman who'd come to the craft service whisked her toward yet another tent. Inside she found none other than Oliver Beck standing beside— "Denz? Is that *you*?"

He'd been transformed. Makeup had taken a turn at him as well, it seemed, and his normally clean-shaven face now had a beard attached. They'd dressed him in a black T-shirt and black slacks, making him look like a mob enforcer given the abundant muscles revealed by the short sleeves.

"Ms. Simmons, I'm Oliver Beck. Thank you for agreeing to be the last-minute fill-in."

"I'm not sure I agreed as much as I was commandeered."

"Same," Denz mused, staring at her.

"You two know each other?" Oliver asked, shifting his attention between them.

Denz quickly filled Oliver in on how while Claire stood frozen as the awestruck fangirl she was.

"Well, that is a coincidence," Oliver said. "It's nice to meet you, Claire."

"L-likewise."

"So here's the scene and why you two are perfect. Denz is basically playing himself, a bodyguard. He's caught up to his runaway princess, and she's convinced him to give her a brief taste of freedom before she has to return to her duties. Away from everyone else, they've fallen in love, and the scene you're about to do is the goodbye kiss before her family takes her away."

Kiss?

Claire glanced at Denz and then back at Oliver Beck, aware of the flush rising up her neck into her cheeks. "Shouldn't the actual actors be doing this?"

Oliver Beck's handsome face twisted into a grimace. "Yes, but both have come down with a stomach bug, so now we're improvising due to the schedule. It won't be a close-up and"—he turned and waved a hand at the head-set-wearing woman who'd found Claire in the van—"we've matched you up really well, I think," he said, taking the sheet of paper the woman handed him and passing it on to Claire. It was a photograph of the actors.

"I'm... You mean I'm the stand-in for *her*?"

Everyone chuckled at Claire's question and the utter disbelief in her tone.

"You don't see the resemblance?" Oliver asked, his gaze twinkling.

To a Hollywood actress known for her beauty and style? "No."

"Trust me, it's there. You'll do just fine. And remember the compensation whenever you get frustrated with me having you repeat things," Oliver continued. "You're saving me, and I'll be sure to pass my gratitude along in the payment. Now, you two ready?"

Claire looked at Denz, expecting him to protest, but realized he looked as uncomfortable as she felt. It was then that she remembered Denz had to work with Oliver professionally at times, so he was probably a little uncomfortable protesting something as simple as a kiss.

But for her…it wasn't just a kiss. It was her *first* kiss… since her last first kiss with Scott. "Wait. Uh, who…does the kissing? I mean, does he o-or—"

"You do it," Oliver said.

Oh, boy. "Uh…"

"Okay," Oliver said, his voice loud and carrying to those around them. "Let's get out there and wrap this up."

"Just remember you're in love and this is the end," the female assistant said to Claire. "One really good kiss and you're done and can go on a shopping spree. Oh, and you can keep the dress. Perks of the timing."

Keep the dress? The designer label on it had made her gasp. She had a pretty good idea of what dresses like this cost.

But maybe it would work for the wedding she'd agreed to attend?

Only if you get this right. I doubt you'll get to keep the dress if you say no.

Everyone turned to head toward the beach where the scene apparently took place, and Claire took a fortifying breath.

"You okay?" Denz asked, pausing as he walked by her.

"Yes. F-fine." She motioned for him to lead the way but startled when he reached out and grasped her hand in his to steady her on the shifting sand.

"Breathe, Claire. It's just a kiss."

A huff of a laugh bubbled out of her chest. "I j-just can't believe this is happening—or that I'm actually going along with it."

"Nice chunk of change up for grabs," he told her. "Does that help offset having to kiss me?"

She couldn't answer that because she honestly wasn't sure of her answer. She didn't imagine kissing Denz would be a chore but—

"Okay," Oliver said from up ahead of them. "So here's the deal, you two know your time is up. Fun is over. Time to get back to reality. That means duty for you," he said to Claire, "and reassignment for you because you've crossed the line."

"Got it," Denz said.

"Denz, you're facing the ocean and turn when you sense her behind you. You'll be filmed from behind and above, which is why close in looks works fine here. Claire, you start off walking but rush the last few steps and throw yourself into his arms and kiss. Now, it's up to you if it's stage kiss or real. Just make it look good. You want to practice a few times? Get a feel for it?"

Practice?

"Sure," Denz said, answering for them both.

"Places!"

Claire jumped at the booming voice, aware of the

sound of the camera-drone taking flight. She met Denz's gaze and blinked. "How did this happen?"

A low chuckle rumbled out of him and soothed her fraught nerves.

"I'm not quite sure myself. So how do you want to do this?"

"Stage," she said automatically. "I-I kiss down, you kiss up?" she asked, remembering her high school theater teacher's instructions when it came to onstage kisses.

"Whatever you want."

Denz turned his back to her and Oliver called action. She took a few steps then picked up speed. Denz turned and she flung herself toward him, lifting her arms, shoes in hand, and smacked them both in the face when the strappy sandals kept speed.

They jerked back before the kiss could even take place and laughed with embarrassment as the crew cracked up.

"All good," Oliver said, smiling himself. "That's why we practice. Try again."

Claire moved back to her appointed position and pulled in a deep breath, reminding herself of the cushion the extra money would give her. That alone calmed her nerves a bit as she took position.

This time when she started toward Denz and raised her arms, she was careful not to swing the shoes so hard. Denz turned and caught her against his chest, and she pulled his head low, giving him an awkward kiss.

"Cut!"

She broke away, embarrassed by her ineptness, and heard Denz murmur something about the third time being the charm.

"Claire?"

She looked up at him and found his brown eyes warm and welcoming. Comforting?

"Relax. It's just me, a friend."

She shook her head, and as though he read her thoughts and realized the importance of her head shake, his gaze widened just a tad.

"Ready?"

Her fangirl crush on Oliver Beck was waning fast.

She took position and looked up to see Denz still watching her. Their gazes locked, and it was a long moment before he turned away to face the ocean once more.

She thought about what Oliver had told her regarding the character she was meant to be. Someone boxed in by responsibilities and expectations, drawn to a man she couldn't have because of who he was and what he did.

Denz was handsome, kind. Caring. He'd proven so several times in the brief time she'd known him. Under different circumstances, maybe…

She inhaled and took a step. Another and another, the last couple a rush to get to him before it was too late and her chance at this moment was forever lost.

Denz turned and caught her against him, and this time she forgot about the stupid shoes and the buzzing drone and the people watching.

She stared up at him, mouths almost touching but not, until she closed her eyes and closed the distance, pressing an urgent kiss to his mouth born of desperation and fear and desire.

Real and pretend.

Denz's arms tightened around her, lifting her against him. In that instant, something changed. He cradled her face with his palm as though cherishing the forbidden moment, the intensity and emotion too close and too real for comfort.

She gasped for breath, and the moment her lips parted,

Denz changed the angle and the kiss deepened. Definitely not fake.

One kiss blended into another, before they slowly drew apart, forehead to forehead, gazing into each other's eyes, until Oliver cut the scene and people clapped.

"That was fantastic," Oliver said.

"Given the significance of the occasion," Denz murmured, "I thought I ought to do it right."

And oh, had he ever. Her knees were weak, her entire body trembled, and though she could probably blame her reaction on the nervousness of filming, she knew to do so would be a lie.

"You two sure you've never done this before?" Oliver asked as he joined them. "I think you filmed better than the actors."

"Easy to do with such a beautiful woman," Denz said.

She managed a weak smile, unsure of how to respond.

"You did a great job today. I expected to be here for hours."

"Thank you," she said.

"Claire, Denz mentioned you went to school with Marsali and Eliza?"

"Um, yeah, I did. Eons ago."

"Well, Marsali has already texted me about how excited she is to see you again. She's usually here on the last day but couldn't make it. She hates that she missed seeing you in action."

Claire smiled at the statement. Glad she hadn't had the added pressure when she was already inordinately thankful for the fact that Tommy was in the craft service van with her father and hadn't witnessed the scene.

She stood there listening to Oliver and Denz talk for several more moments before they all turned to head back toward the tents.

She sensed someone staring at her and searched the crowd gathered behind the barriers. Her stomach twisted into a hard knot when she spotted her son, front and center, his hands gripping the barrier in front of him.

Their gazes locked and Claire could see the upset Tommy wasn't able to hide. She also knew why.

He'd seen her kissing Denz.

Chapter 15

Claire rushed to wardrobe to change and then wadded the elegant dress and its bag in her arms for the mad dash to craft service and the van where her son should have been during shooting.

She got to the van feeling sweaty and chaotic and earned raised eyebrows from her father.

"Something wrong?" Tom asked.

"Uh, no. I was just rushing to get back here so I could help. I didn't want to leave you alone for too long. Where's Tommy?"

"Haven't seen him. He went to watch you."

She stowed the dress inside the van for safekeeping. The creator would probably see such a thing as sacrilege considering it probably cost more than the van itself. "Thanks. Dad, do you need me? I kind of have a headache. I think I'll try to find Tommy and head home."

"You go ahead. We have everything covered. Lunch rush is over."

"Thanks, Dad. I'll do better next time."

"Not a problem. I've wound up an extra like that a

time or two myself. It just means you're in the business now."

In the business? Hardly. "If you see Tommy, tell him to wait here and text me?"

"Will do."

Claire left the van and meandered through the food area but didn't see her son. From there she took advantage of the fact she was a face "on set" so to speak and looked around there to see if maybe Tommy had snuck past the guards.

She was starting to panic, especially when she hadn't heard from her father, when she spotted someone sitting a ways down the beach. Her instincts put her feet into motion, and within moments, she was able to see well enough to know that it was Tommy.

She approached cautiously, unsure of his mood. "Hey. I've been looking everywhere for you. Are you ready to go home?"

"To Virginia?"

Oh, that didn't bode well. "No. To Grandpa's. He said we could leave if you're ready."

Tommy set his jaw, nostrils flaring as he tried to control his emotions.

"I want to go home."

"Tommy—"

"He's not Dad."

"Denz? No, he's not."

"Then why did you kiss him?"

"You know why. You heard exactly what happened and how I wound up in that situation, and that kiss… It was acting. I got paid to do it. Quite a bit, I might add. Money we need right now."

"I know what you're doing."

She dropped to her knees on the sand beside him and shifted sideways to sit. "What do you think I'm doing?"

"You're trying to get rid of him. You sold all of his stuff. You're gonna sell the house even though I don't want you to. Now you're kissing that guy. It's like you're glad Dad's gone."

"Tommy, *no*. That's not true at all."

"It didn't look like a fake kiss."

Because it hadn't been. Not by the end. But Tommy wasn't mature enough to handle such adult matters when it came to the enormity of the first kiss after losing a spouse, nor how Denz had made it special for her. "Denz and I… We tried to make it look real so we could get it over with and not have to keep doing it."

"So you don't like him?"

"Oh, Tommy, I don't even know him. Denz seems nice but—"

"It's only been a year."

A year since Scott's death, but nearly three since they were on the same continent. "I know." She shifted and wrapped her arm around his shoulders. "You have no reason to worry, okay? I'm sorry the scene hurt you. For what it's worth, I didn't know I'd be kissing anyone, much less Denz. But rest assured we're just…friends."

"For real?"

"For real. Now, are you ready to go? I want to scrub this stuff off my face and enjoy some waves. Maybe try out the new skimboards Grandpa picked up? What do you say?"

―――――

LATER THAT EVENING, Denz headed out for a run when he spotted Tommy outside in the hammock with his headset on. "Hey, you up for a workout?"

The kid looked surprised by the question, then wary, but shrugged.

"I guess."

"Go ask your mom if you can come with me to the gym. I'll wait."

Tommy went into the house and Denz stretched while he waited. A minute passed and Claire emerged, dressed in pink shorts and a white top that showcased the bronze sheen of her afternoon at the beach.

She approached him and tucked her hands into her back pockets. "The gym?"

"Is that okay? I thought I'd show him around. Introduce him to people. Maybe work off some of that frustration."

"That's nice of you. Thanks."

"My pleasure." Awkward silence filled the space between them, and he took a step closer. "Claire, are we okay?"

"Of course."

"You're sure?"

A small smile broke over her face and she averted her gaze.

"Let's just say that wasn't how I expected the first kiss after my husband to go. I mean, the people and cameras and craziness."

"I hope it wasn't too unpleasant for you."

A rosy hue flooded her cheeks. "Fishing for compliments?"

"Maybe I am."

"It wasn't *awful*," she said, her tone teasing.

A laugh bubbled out of her at his expression and he welcomed the sound.

"It was very nice, Denz."

Nice? Nice was the kiss of death. Was *very* nice different? "Well, you let me know if you decide you want to practice some more. Get it perfected for next time."

"Next time?" she asked, eyes wide.

"That way you won't be nervous when you do decide to start dating again," he said, his gaze shifting to the screen door as her son burst out of the house.

Claire stepped back, cheeks rosy, and told them to be careful, waving after they climbed into his SUV.

"So," Denz said as he got them rolling. "Did you apologize to your mom?"

"Yeah."

"And?"

"She said I have to go back to grief counseling."

"That's not a bad idea."

"It's just a bunch of losers talking about feelings and sharing how they suck."

"That sounds a little harsh," Denz said to the kid. "Would it help to know I've sat in a session or two myself?"

"You have?"

He nodded as he made the stops and turns to get them out of the little neighborhood. "The military uses counselors. And after shootings and the like, private security companies like I work for use them to make sure their guys are ready to get back in the field. So, yeah, I have."

"Did it help?"

He drove them to Dow and headed toward the far end of the island. "Yeah. It did. You just have to have an open mind."

Tommy stared out his window, quiet for a time.

"Would you let me get on my game and see if my friends are there?"

"No." He shot the kid a look. "Not without your mom's permission."

Tommy shifted in the bucket seat, looking glum.

"I'm sorry I hurt her, you know. It's just I knew where she'd put it, and it's nice to talk to my dad's friends. They tell me stories about him."

"Your mom doesn't do that?"

"Not really. I don't want to make her sad, so I don't ask. I hear her crying sometimes," he said, face turned to the window. "I want to help her but I don't know how."

That was a big admission from a kid in pain. A kid who wanted to be a man but wasn't. "The best way you can help her is to stay out of trouble. You realize that, right?"

"I guess. I don't mean to get into trouble, it just sort of happens."

Denz chuckled. "That kind of stuff usually happens when you're not where you're supposed to be, doing what you're supposed to be doing."

"Do you like my mom?"

The change in topic was so abrupt Denz's first instinct was to lie. "Uh, yeah. I like her fine."

"That's not what I meant. The date to the wedding… Is it really a date?"

"Not as far as your mom is concerned." Denz was glad to see the building housing the gym up ahead.

"So she doesn't know you like her?"

"Why all the questions?"

"Because she's my mom. Are you going to tell her?"

He didn't have to think long on that one. "I'm a friend, Tommy. That's all."

"But you like her?"

"Tommy, being an adult, being a man and a productive

member of society," Denz said pointedly, "means looking out for others, even if it means not getting what you want. I…like your mom," he admitted, "but she needs something I can't give her."

"What's that mean?"

His grip tightened on the steering wheel. "It means she needs someone to lean on and help her while she figures things out."

"But you just said you're her friend."

"Yeah, I am but—"

"So isn't that what a friend does?"

Chapter 16

Claire spent the next hour or so fine-tuning her resume and searching online for jobs, but when it came to applying, she couldn't make herself hit the button. Should she apply here...or in Virginia?

Since that was the mental debate taking place, she knew she couldn't put off talking to her father any longer, though she wasn't sure how to bring it up.

A long walk through the neighborhood brought back memories and longings for a return to the area where she'd grown up, but before she made the final decision, she needed to settle some things.

Near the pier, Claire decided to call her real estate friend to see if she'd had a chance to take a look at the house. The discussion hit the highlights and pointed toward a sale, furthering Claire's thoughts toward moving back to Carolina Cove.

She found a spot on one of the swings and stared out at the ocean, letting the soothing sounds of the surf and the birds flow through her.

Moving was always a big deal, but moving to another

state, into a new school, was infinitely more difficult than simply moving to a new neighborhood. But as her friend had told her, the market was hot now, but that could change as quickly as the economy. She needed to decide, the sooner the better.

Claire finished her drink and tossed her cup in the trash before heading back to the house. Ten minutes later, she entered the living room, and Tommy was nowhere to be seen. "They're not back yet?"

"Not yet."

"That's good, actually."

"Oh? Why's that?"

She hesitated and shifted her weight from foot to foot. "Dad, um, there's something I'd like to talk to you about."

Her father clicked off the television and gave her his full attention, even though he was stretched out in his favorite recliner.

"Um, so I've been thinking about something. A-about selling the house and moving. Maybe…moving here."

"Why?"

She blinked at him. "Why?"

"Are you just wanting to move back, or are things that bad financially?"

A huff of air left her lungs at her father's intuitiveness. It wouldn't do her any good to blame Scott, not now. She had to own her part, which included not arguing harder against the purchases they hadn't been able to afford. Sixty-thousand-dollar trucks and Jeeps, the homes, Harley… "The, uh, house has a lot of equity. I talked to a friend in real estate, and she thinks I could get enough out of it to pay off all my debt," she said honestly. "Also, there's Tommy."

"What about Tommy? Is something wrong with him?"

"What? No, nothing's *wrong* with him, it's just… I told

you Tommy hasn't been able to find his groove since Scott was killed, and I think he needs a solid male role model. I thought maybe you'd like to spend more time with him."

"He is at that age," her father said with a nod.

"Right. So, yeah, that's what I'm thinking. You know, if you wouldn't mind us moving here."

"Why would I mind?"

She inhaled and seated herself on the edge of the coffee table. Why? Did he hear his tone of voice? "Because there are times when I think you hate me, Dad."

"Don't be silly."

"Hate is hardly something to joke about."

Her father swung the reclining footrest in with a bang and shot out of the chair. He stalked into the kitchen and then turned to glare at her.

"You know good and well I don't hate you. You're my daughter and you're welcome here any time."

"You mean we were welcome to stay in the apartment?" she asked, clarifying.

"That again? Claire, you should've called first if it bothers you so much to stay here in the house with me."

"Dad, that's not what I meant."

"Don't know why I'm surprised you don't like it when you made it clear at seventeen that you couldn't stand—"

"Oh, for the love of— Enough! Dad, that was *fourteen* years ago! Scott was the father of my baby and I was in love. Did you really expect me to stay?"

"Yes! Yes, I did! I expected you to use the brains God gave you."

"To raise Tommy alone?"

"You wouldn't have been alone. Your mother and I would've helped you."

"But Scott was his *father*. Scott wanted to be a father and *you*… Dad, you wanted to control my life and I couldn't let you. Give me some credit for being *like* you in that way."

"That boy took you away from us and then abandoned you."

"He *deployed*, Dad, not abandoned. Big difference."

Her father wiped a hand over his head and paced the floor.

"You should've stayed with us instead of dragging that baby all over the country."

"I wanted to be with my *husband*."

"You broke your mother's heart. She never got to see much of Tommy, and now here you are talking about moving back—something she always dreamed you'd do—and she's not even here to see it."

Her father's voice cracked with emotion, and the impact hit Claire in the very depths of her soul.

She shoved herself up off the coffee table and stood on trembling legs. "I know. And I'm sorry for that. But it's not too late for you to know Tommy and help influence his life—unless you keep acting like this, in which case I might as well stay in Virginia."

She turned to head outside, needing fresh air and space and the soothing sounds of the waves crashing in the distance.

"Claire."

She squeezed her eyes closed and paused on the tile floor, waiting for another barrage. "What?"

"I'd like it if you were closer. I hope you and Tommy do move back. You can use the apartment once Denz goes back to work in a week or two. It's yours for as long as you need it."

"Thank you."

"No need to thank me. I'm sorry I made you feel unwelcome. I just didn't like losing my baby girl to someone I knew couldn't take care of her. Not the way I could."

Her shoulders slumped, and she wished for the millionth time that her father understood her reasons for doing what she'd done. "Scott did his best, Dad. Tommy and I never lacked for anything. He was a great father and a good soldier. He was a good man—not perfect but *good*. Isn't that all that matters?"

"We didn't like losing our baby girl," he said, his voice gruff.

"That's just it, Dad. You didn't lose me. You gained a son and a grandson."

Her father was silent a long moment.

"Will selling the house help settle your accounts? Do you need to borrow money?"

"Yes, it will—and, no, I don't need money but thanks. Once it sells, everything will be fine."

"You'll let me know if I can help you?"

She swallowed hard and managed a smile. "I will. Right now the biggest problem will be telling Tommy. He knows I've been thinking about it and… He's not happy about leaving his friends."

"You have to do what's best for the two of you. You can't let a boy decide that."

"I know."

"Do you want me to talk to him?"

"No. I'll tell him."

"You're sure?"

"Yeah. I'm sure. Thanks. For letting us use the apartment." Claire turned and made her way through the kitchen to the screen door, uncaring that it softly banged behind her.

She paced the porch several times before finally settling into the porch swing, giving it a rough push.

Lights flashed in the driveway and Denz's rental appeared. It was dusk, and she dreaded dinnertime spent at the table because she was emotionally drained once more.

Maybe she should splurge and take Tommy out to eat? But how did that treat factor into Tommy's most recent bad behavior? Would it be a red flag to him that would send him into a mood?

Doors slammed shut and she watched Tommy approach. Her gaze narrowed, taking in the rare smile that flashed over his face in response to something Denz said. Her son was sweat-soaked and visibly tired, but…happy? "Look at you. I take it things went well?"

"Yeah. Denz introduced me to someone named Mac. He's one of the owners, and Mac got me a pass so I can go workout whenever, and I joined the youth weightlifting program."

She blinked. "Mac Jones?"

"Yeah, that's him. He's great…and the program is for kids my age," Tommy said.

"It's monitored," Denz added softly. "The guys are all volunteers. Firemen, law enforcement. They teach the kids proper form and how to do things the right way. It's a great way to get to know some other kids on the island."

"Yeah," Tommy said again. "If it's okay, I'm going to meet a couple of them tomorrow to hang out and surf."

"Uh, maybe," she said, knowing the local kids surfed in groups but struggling with the concept of Tommy suddenly being one of them.

"I'm gonna go shower. I stink. Is dinner soon?"

"Go. I'll make sure something is ready when you get out," she said, completely blown away by her talkative son. He hadn't said that many words since…

Before his dad's death.

Tommy went into the house with a bang of the door, and Denz stayed where he was, just off the porch.

"I should go shower, too. Have a good evening, Claire."

One minute she was on the swing, the next she was up and rushing toward him in a repeat of the movie scene on the beach.

Denz heard her and turned in time to catch her against him, and she lifted her arms to pull his head low, lifting her face, her lips, to kiss him.

This kiss was different. Freer. With no one around and no cameras rolling, she pressed her lips to his and put every ounce of thankfulness and warmth she felt into the embrace. Lingering over the caress.

Denz wrapped one arm around her waist and lifted her up, carrying her until her feet hit the steps and she found her footing. She smiled against his lips, realizing he'd leveled their heights.

The kissing continued until a light flicked on in the darkened house behind them, and she pulled away, biting her lower lip as she stared at him.

Denz tilted his head, gaze narrowed on her. Tall and strong and silent. Sexy.

"What was that for?" he asked softly.

"F-for helping Tommy."

"He's a good kid."

"He is. I haven't seen him that happy and carefree in…ages."

"Claire?"

"Yeah?"

"Thank you."

"For what?"

"That's the best thank you I've ever gotten."

She couldn't stop the smile from forming. "I, um,

should get inside and get something ready for Tommy. Do you have food? Would you like to join us?"

That was the polite thing to do, wasn't it? Invite someone for dinner? Even though technically dinner usually came first, then the kissing. She would think about the consequences of what she'd done later, but for now, she was okay with it. After all, what harm was a thank-you kiss when they'd already shared one on the set?

"I need a shower."

"Of course."

"Ten minutes?"

Realizing he'd just accepted her invitation, she nodded. "Yeah."

"I'll be in soon."

She watched him turn and go, his long strides carrying him rapidly across the lawn to the stairs leading up to the apartment.

She turned and placed her hand on the screen door to open it but paused when the awareness of what she'd done kicked in.

She'd kissed Denz. As a thank-you and because she'd wanted to. And it had felt good.

But what happened now?

Chapter 17

Denz wasn't sure what to expect when he arrived at the house post shower. Claire's kiss had surprised him, but it wasn't an unpleasant one, especially not when he thought about Tommy's words about being her friend.

Claire was a smart woman. She knew his job, knew his situation and presence in town were temporary. If she was okay with kissing him, he certainly wasn't going to stop her. He didn't know a man who would.

He grabbed a bottle of wine on his way out the door to take as a gift because it seemed to be the thing to do when invited to dinner. On the porch, he tamped down a surprising case of nerves that appeared out of nowhere, reminding him of the time he'd asked Rachel Tolliver to the sixth-grade dance.

On the one hand, he could take Claire's kiss at face value. She had been grateful that he'd helped out Tommy, and she'd expressed her thanks physically.

On the other hand, he could take it as a sign the filmed kiss had stirred up interest, and she used her happiness as an excuse to explore the potential.

But if that was the case… He wasn't sure how he felt about it given the living arrangement he had with her father. Especially when Tom would undoubtedly frown at a relationship that could only be casual since Denz would be leaving to head back to work very soon.

"Hey, almost ready," she said after Denz knocked and opened the screen door.

He let himself inside and noted Tom's bushy eyebrows shooting high at the sight of the gift. "You've fed me a few times, so I wanted to contribute something," he said simply.

"Thanks. That'll go great with the steaks," she said. "Dad just put them on the grill."

"Hey, Denz, are you going to the gym tomorrow?" Tommy asked as he walked down the hallway.

"Tommy, I'm sure Denz doesn't want to be your chauffeur," she said.

"I am," Denz said to Tommy, "and it's fine," he said to Claire. "Any time I'm heading that way, he's welcome to go with me. How about that?"

Both mother and son smiled at him while Denz sensed Tom's stare.

Dinner was delicious. Tom knew how to perfectly grill a steak, and along with fresh veggies, dinner rolls, and pudding Claire whipped up for dessert, Denz ate his fill. He enjoyed listening to Tommy tell his mother about the kids he'd met at the gym and sensed Claire's happiness as her kid kept the conversation from ever lagging.

"I'm going to go take my walk before it gets any later," Tom said, shoving himself back from the table.

"I'll clean up," Claire said.

"Tommy, you help your mother," Tom said.

"Okay."

Tom seemed surprised by the kid's quick agreement, but the man left without commenting further.

Denz stood and carried his plate to the sink.

"Oh, leave that. We'll get it," Claire said.

"That's not how I was raised to leave a table," Denz said, hoping Tommy listened.

With all three of them clearing, loading the dishwasher, and wiping things down, it didn't take long to clean up.

"Can I watch TV now?" Tommy asked.

"Yeah, go ahead. We're finished here."

Claire took the tablecloth outside to shake it off and Denz followed her. "Dinner was great."

"It was, wasn't it?"

"So was the company."

She stilled and he watched her closely while she stopped shaking the tablecloth and held it in front of her. Her teeth sank into her lower lip while she folded the material.

"Denz…"

He waited, watching her. When she didn't continue, he stretched out his hands and grabbed the sides of the tablecloth, letting his grip slide to the opposite ends from hers. He lifted them and carried them up, fingers brushing hers in the process. "Something wrong?"

"No. No, I'm fine. I'm just… Was that weird? For you? What I did?"

"It wasn't weird at all. Was it for you?" He let her take the material but didn't move away from her.

"A little. I'm…not sorry, though."

"I'm glad to hear that."

"But I don't want it to be… I don't want you to think that… What I mean to say is I'm…"

"We're good, Claire. And the shoulder I offered is still available any time you need it."

"So we're…friends."

"Yes."

"Good. That's…good."

"Are we still on for the wedding?" he asked, hoping the change of subject might remove some of the tension he saw in her beautiful features.

"Yes. I can't wait. I haven't looked forward to anything as much in a long time."

He grinned at her words, wishing she looked forward to going with *him* as much as she did rubbing shoulders with Oliver and seeing her school friends again. "I'm sure it will be spectacular, especially with Eliza Hayes planning it."

"It will be nice to reconnect with everyone again, especially since I'm going to move ba—"

She broke off so abruptly he frowned. "Come again?"

"I, um"—she glanced toward the house, lowering her voice—"talked with my father this evening while you and Tommy were gone. I've…decided to move us back to Carolina Cove."

"But you haven't told Tommy?"

"No. He knows I've been thinking about it but not that I've decided for sure."

"Maybe the time at the gym will help the transition," he said. "He seemed to get along okay with the kids there and is excited about hanging out."

"I'm glad. I can't thank you enough for that. For taking him and introducing him… It means a lot."

"You're welcome." He took a step closer but then stopped himself. "I guess I should go and let you settle in for the evening."

Claire stared up at him, her eyes sparkling as she nodded.

"Have a good night."

Denz turned and headed down the steps and across the yard. He didn't let himself glance back until he made it to the stairs leading up to the apartment. Claire had gone back inside and stood at the kitchen window at the sink, the light overhead giving her blond hair a bright shimmer.

Tommy's question came back to him then, filtering through Denz's brain. Friends let friends lean on them. They helped them.

And while he was in town, he planned on letting Claire do that...in whatever form she needed.

CLAIRE DECIDED to wait until the following afternoon to tell Tommy about her decision. She'd told her father they wouldn't be joining him today at work and instead woke Tommy up and took him to the battleship. The tour was self-guided, and they spent hours climbing and reading and exploring every accessible part of the ship.

"We're moving, aren't we?"

Tommy's quietly posed question drew her attention to where her son stood looking at the impossibly tiny room designated as officers' quarters.

"Yes."

"I knew it. You've been acting weird all day."

"I haven't acted weird. Have I?" she asked.

Tommy shot her a look and she inhaled and moved closer to where he stood. "Okay, fine. Maybe I have, but only because I don't want you to be upset, but I know you're going to be at least a little. Just, please remember that I've looked at every option and...I think this is the best for us."

"Me, too."

Tommy's response couldn't have shocked her more. "Excuse me?"

"I think you're right."

"Okay. Who are you and what have you done with my kid?"

"Mom," he said, rolling his eyes.

"I—I'm not sure what to say except I'm glad you feel that way."

"Denz said that part of being a man is doing stuff I might not like because it's important for someone else."

Denz said, huh?

"I don't want to move, but I get that the house is too much, and I can tell Grandpa is lonely."

"Yeah. Grandpa… I talked to Grandpa and he says we can have the apartment as long as we need. Would you like that? Living so close to Grandpa and the beach?"

"It would be okay. Grandpa's already said I could work with him in the summers and after school and save up for a car."

A car? Oh, that was a reality that wasn't all that far away, wasn't it? "When did he say that?"

"The other day."

"Sounds like you've made some plans of your own."

Tommy shrugged. "Maybe."

She placed her hand on Tommy's bony shoulder and gently squeezed, wondering how her six-pound ten-ounce baby boy had grown so much. "I wouldn't do this if I didn't think it was best for us. You know that, right?"

"Yeah, I guess. If we move, do I still have to go to therapy?"

"Yes. Sorry, kiddo, but that's nonnegotiable."

"Denz says he's gone to therapy."

He had? "Oh?"

"For the shooting and the military and stuff. He said it's not a big deal and I need an open mind."

"Does that make therapy more tolerable now?" she asked, "knowing that men like Denz talk to people about what they've been through?"

"I guess. It definitely doesn't make it seem like loserville."

"Well, there is that, I suppose," she said, smiling.

"I'm hungry."

"When are you not hungry? Come on, let's get moving so we can feed you."

"Mom?"

"Yeah?"

Claire turned back and waited as Tommy studied her.

"I'm sorry I've been a pain. I know I said I was sorry before but…I really am."

Her heart squeezed from the vulnerability she saw in Tommy's eyes. "Thank you. That means a lot to me, Tommy."

She wanted to hug him, but she knew his teenage mind would probably view that as ruining the moment. So instead she smiled and led the way toward the next passageway and eventually made their way out of the ship, passing on the fast-food options available for something more substantial. Claire drove them into downtown Wilmington to the Riverwalk and the waterfront restaurants there, deciding the momentous day needed a little extra splurge.

They chose a waterfront restaurant and lucked into a shaded table.

"Claire? Is that you?"

Claire turned at the sound of her name and spotted Marsali Jones Beck, easily recognizable with her gorgeous curly hair. "Oh! Hi, Marsali. Yeah, it's me."

The woman hurried toward Claire and Claire and Tommy both stood.

"Oh, my goodness! It's so good to run into you," Marsali said, giving Claire a warm hug.

Claire was aware of the large, imposing man nearby and remembered him as the bodyguard from the shoot the other day. "Marsali, this is my son, Tommy," Claire said, inordinately proud of her son when he remembered his manners.

"Nice to meet you," Tommy said.

"And you. So handsome," Marsali said to Claire. "So, tell me. Are you going to be in town long?"

"Actually," Claire said, "we're celebrating. Tommy and I have officially decided to move back. I still have to sell our house in Virginia, but Carolina Cove is going to be home again soon."

"Oh, that's wonderful! Your father is probably over the moon. I was so sorry to hear about your mom and…your husband. Claire…"

"Thank you," she said, wrapping her arm around Tommy's narrow waist. "We're doing okay. Right, bub?"

Tommy nodded.

"Here, take my number," Marsali said, pulling a card from her purse. "We need to get together. You, me, Eliza… She won't be free until after Mac and V's wedding, but maybe we can get together next week?"

"I'd like that. And if there's anything I can do to help, count me in. I've always loved weddings."

"I'll tell Eliza," Marsali said. "She may take you up on that."

"I'd be happy to help."

"Mom, I'll be back," Tommy said, excusing himself.

Claire watched as he made his way toward the restrooms.

"So…you know Denz," Marsali said.

Claire blinked at the sudden change in topic and nodded. "I do," Claire said. "He's renting my father's apartment while he's on medical leave."

"And bringing you to the wedding."

Claire felt her face heat. "He didn't want to go alone."

"Oliver said you two had some major chemistry during filming."

Claire shook her head. "We are just friends."

Marsali looked disappointed. "Too bad. Denz is a good guy. Hardworking, dedicated."

"Temporary," Claire added, reminding herself and Marsali.

"Ah, yeah, I suppose he is that," Marsali with a wrinkle of her nose. "But that statement… Does that mean you've thought about dating again?"

"Oh. Marsali…"

"I know it's hard, but if you're ready, I'd love to help you with that. Free of charge. Just say the word. I'd be honored to set you up, and with you moving back to Carolina Cove, it would be a great way of meeting people and…making new friends?"

Denz had warned Claire that Marsali would be all about setting her up. At the time, she'd laughed off the idea, but now…maybe it was time to *think* about moving forward?

"You're considering it. I can tell," Marsali said, her tone excited. "Oh, Claire, please let me help you?"

Chapter 18

During the next couple of days, Claire and Tommy worked mornings to midafternoons with Claire's father. Denz spent his days at PT, fishing off the pier, or on the beach reading and took Tommy to the gym in the evenings. The kid's attitude seemed to be improving, and Denz even caught a few smiles.

Earlier at the gym, Tommy told the kids in the group about moving to Carolina Cove, and the news was met with enthusiasm. Tommy was invited to the beach with the kids the following day to swim and hang out again, and the kid quickly agreed.

Denz sat on the apartment steps to enjoy the evening breeze and noted that Claire still wasn't back. Tommy had told him Marsali and Eliza had accepted Claire's offer to pitch in on wedding prep, but Denz figured the ladies were simply using that as an excuse to hang out as women tended to do.

His phone buzzed and he frowned when Claire's number appeared. "Hey. You have too much fun and need a ride home?"

"Denz, something happened. I'm fine. We're all fine. B-but there was a man… Can you come get me? I-I'm too shaky to drive and I don't want to wake D-dad…"

He gripped the phone so hard he heard the plastic crack. "Where are you?"

"Eliza's house. Do you know—"

"I'll be right there. Stay with Oliver. I'm on my way." Denz had liked the idea of Claire hanging out with her friends, knowing she needed that time to reconnect. But obviously being in close proximity to Oliver and Marsali had put Claire in danger.

He grabbed his keys and raced across Carolina Cove before getting stopped by police when he turned down their street. Lights flashed up and down the area, but mostly at the end near Carter Hayes's home. His pulse raced at the sight, and Denz lowered his window as a cop approached.

He had to show his ID, but Oliver or someone had alerted the police to Denz's impending arrival. The cop allowed Denz to pass, and he jerked the vehicle to a stop and hurried toward Carter and Eliza's house.

Carter stood on the porch talking to yet another cop, while more searched the area with flashlights. "What happened?" Denz asked Carter when he got close enough to be heard.

"Oliver and Marsali had an unwelcome visitor tonight. The girls finished the wedding prep and walked over to the house to take a tour of the remodel only to discover they weren't alone."

Denz's heart thumped hard in his chest as adrenaline surged at the news. He jogged up the steps to where Carter waited.

"Thanks for your help," Carter said to the cop before turning to Denz. "Come on, everyone is inside."

Carter led the way into his home, and Denz followed on the man's heels, impatient in his desire to get to Claire.

Oliver and Lincoln stood in the kitchen with two more officers, all of them wearing dark expressions. Denz's hands clenched when he didn't see the ladies.

"Denz," Oliver said.

"Mr. Beck," Denz greeted, adding a nod. "You've had some excitement."

The ladies emerged from a room behind them. Marsali immediately moved to Oliver's side. Eliza and Amelia joined their husbands respectively, and Claire stopped somewhat awkwardly a few steps away from Denz, arms wrapped tight around herself because she trembled from head to toe. "Hey," he said softly. "Are you okay?"

"That man scared us all to death," Marsali said. "We were looking at the house, and teasing Claire because she'd *finally* agreed to let me match her, and there he was."

Match her? So Claire wanted to date, huh?

"Yeah, just when I think I'm ready to date again, the world's like, let's send in a crazy guy."

Everyone laughed at Claire's wobbly attempt at humor. Everyone but Denz, who couldn't stand the sight of her trembling like a frightened puppy. He shoved his reservations aside and closed the distance between them. He wrapped an arm around her shoulders and drew her close, very aware of the gazes watching them.

"Please don't think it's a sign that you shouldn't," Marsali said.

"The guy's in custody," Oliver told Denz, bringing them back to the seriousness of the moment. "The police say he appears to be alone, but they're giving everything a thorough check."

"Where was Bruce?" Denz asked.

"He'd walked over with us and was waiting downstairs," Marsali said. "We screamed and he came running but—"

"The guy made a grab for Marsali and Claire shoved him away," Amelia said, her arms tightening around Lincoln's waist.

"She was so brave," Marsali said tearfully. "Claire, I can't thank you enough."

"I'm glad I was able to help," Claire said.

"Attic, closets, and storage areas are clear," a voice said over the radios worn by the officers.

"Second floor clear," stated another voice.

"Where are Mac and V?" Denz asked. "Piper?"

"Mac had already left to take V home," Lincoln said. "He's probably trying to get back and wondering what's happening."

"I'll call him," Carter said, pulling out his cell. "And Piper's asleep at Linc's with the baby," he said in response to Denz's question about his daughter. "Breanne and Brendan are with them. They're locked up tight with a cop watching the doors."

"Tomorrow is going to be a *looong* day," Marsali murmured. "There's no sleeping after all of this."

"I'm so glad we made V go home early," Eliza said. "Maybe she won't find out until the morning. I don't think any of us will be able to shut our eyes."

Oliver kissed his wife's head and squeezed her against him.

"Denz, I'd like to talk to you first thing in the morning if you're free."

Denz nodded. "You got it. I'll help any way I can."

"Be thinking of ways to lock everything down. The street will be gated full-time from now on," Oliver said. "We've been leaving it up during the day for the construction crews as they work on the house and only closing it at night."

The house Oliver referred to was actually three homes at the end of the street, which were being redesigned and connected into one large one complete with a guest house, massive garage, housekeeping quarters, and all the bells and whistles. Oliver and Marsali had purchased the homes in order to be close to her brother and the friends, and the work was in the final stages of completion.

"I'm thinking the gate should be guarded, not just keyed, but that still leaves the water side accessible. The police found a boat, but they're still trying to confirm if it belongs to the guy and his motive."

"Someone patrolling and keeping an eye on things twenty-four seven wouldn't be a bad idea," Denz said, nodding. "Maybe another dog or two as well, even if they're just pets."

"Piper will be happy about that," Carter said. "She's wanted a dog ever since she met Ginger," he said, referring to Marsali's foster.

"Maybe while you're here in town you could help me get things sorted out? Come up with something compre-hensive?" Oliver asked Denz.

"I'd be happy to," Denz said. "We can talk about it tomorrow."

"Yes, tomorrow. I don't want to think about it anymore." Marsali leaned her head on Oliver's chest. "I've never been so scared."

"Denz will help us get squared away," Oliver said.

"Thank you, Denz," Marsali said.

"My pleasure, Mrs. B. If Claire is finished giving her statement," he said to the cop seemingly in charge, "I'd like to get her home."

For the first time since the ladies had entered, Denz

allowed himself to really look at Claire. She wore some sort of one-piece shorts outfit, her long legs looking longer because of the length—or rather lack thereof—and the strappy heels she wore on her slim feet.

He couldn't imagine her taking someone on in those things, but he was glad she was able to protect her friend, even though she shouldn't have had to.

"We have all we need," the cop said. "If not, I'll be in touch. And if you think of anything else, you call us."

Denz reluctantly released her when Claire moved to accept the card the cop handed her and nodded at the man. "I will. Thank you."

The officers moved toward the front of the house to leave, and Marsali, Eliza, and Amelia surrounded Claire in a group hug.

Goodbyes were said, and Claire sniffled.

"Let's get you home." Denz shook hands with Oliver and walked Claire to his rental. He helped her inside, but when she sat just there and stared at the multitude of flashing lights that had now been joined by camera crews, he tugged the seat belt into place and latched it over her.

He got them turned around and heading in the right direction, and once the police lights were behind them, he gently tugged on her forearm and lifted her hand to his lips. Her fingers were icy, and he held them to his chest to warm.

The summer traffic plucked his last nerve, but finally Denz pulled into Tom's and cut the engine, reluctant to let go of Claire long enough to round the vehicle. "Come on, let's get you inside. Where are your keys?"

Claire fumbled in her purse and produced a set of shiny keys he took from her trembling hand. The house was mostly dark, but Tom had left a light on in the living room.

Denz watched as Claire stumbled her way to the couch and dropped down to sit like she couldn't take another step. He set the keys on the coffee table before lowering himself to the surface to remove her shoes. "I don't know how you don't break an ankle in these."

She didn't speak. One shoe dropped and then he worked his fingers over the straps of the other and it dropped as well. "Claire?"

"I c-can't stop shaking," she said. "Why c-can't I s-stop shaking?"

He shifted off the coffee table onto the couch beside her and pulled her against him. "It's the adrenaline. Fight or flight. And probably more than a little shock."

Denz ran his hand up and down her back, softly, slowly, hoping it soothed her.

She turned her face into his chest and he kissed her head. "It'll stop soon. You're okay, Claire."

"He was going to hurt her. He saw us and started yelling, and then he zeroed in on Marsali and... You should've seen his eyes. The l-look he h-had."

Denz knew exactly what she referred to. Certain men —dangerous men—tended to have the same crazed look. Dark, beady, wild. Whatever the descriptive, their eyes were terrifying, and Denz hated that Claire now had them seared into her memory because of the night. "But he didn't. You stopped him."

"But...Tommy. All I could think of was Tommy. He's lost his d-dad. And if the man... If he'd... If *I*... Tommy would've been alone. What would he d-do?"

"Everyone is safe," he whispered. "Tommy is safe. *You* are safe," he said, stressing each word.

She slid her arms around him and her head stayed buried against him.

"Don't let go."

Denz closed his eyes, barely able to breathe because of the anger coursing through him that someone had scared Claire so badly that she was reduced to the quivering woman he held. "I won't."

"I m-mean it," she whispered again, her breath hot on his chest through his shirt. "Please d-don't let go."

He squeezed her tighter and then shifted and turned her so that she sat on his lap with him cuddling her, head tucked and body curled around him so tightly her knees dug into his ribs. "I'm right here. I won't let go."

At least…not until he was forced to.

Chapter 19

Claire opened her eyes and blinked, confused by everything. The bright light streaming through the window sheers blinded her, and it took a moment for her to remember she wasn't in Virginia but in Carolina Cove. At her father's. In the living room curled up on…Denz?

Claire gasped and the noise must have woken Denz, because his arms tightened around her and his mahogany gaze locked on to hers.

Claire felt her heart tug at the sleep-sexy smile that formed on his lips.

"Morning, beautiful. How do you feel?"

How did she feel? Stupid. She tensed at the memories flooding back. Marsali and the girls, the man…the screaming and fear and chaos. "I can't believe you… You should've left me here a-and gone to bed."

"I don't break promises, sweetheart."

Her panicked request for him to hold her and not let go sounded in her head, and she cringed at the implications. They'd already shared a kiss that had nothing to do with filming and everything to do with wanting to—and now this? He'd slept on the couch, upright, and held her all night? "I'm sorry. I-I mean, thank you but…I'm sorry."

"No need to be sorry."

"I guess I was kind of a mess."

"You had reason to be a mess."

She unclenched her fingers from his shirt, where she'd apparently gripped it all night given the wrinkles, and shoved the hair from her face. Why him? Why couldn't the guy in her father's apartment be some everyday Joe who worked nine to five and didn't carry a gun and run toward trouble on a regular basis? "I'm pretty sure you've faced much worse. I doubt you've ever…well, you know."

"Wanted to hold on to someone? I have."

"Oh."

Denz's admission didn't make her feel better, though. Because him holding her and whispering to her was exactly what she'd wanted. What she'd needed. Even though for the last year she'd told herself she would be perfectly fine going it alone. "Dad will be up soon."

Denz shifted and pressed a hand to her back to steady her as she shoved herself upright on his lap.

Scooting across to the couch cushion took even more effort, but she did so and blamed the flush she felt rising into her face on the summer sun blasting through the windows.

Denz wasn't going to be around in the future, and just because she'd decided she was ready to date didn't mean she could allow herself to depend on him now.

"I need to grab a shower before I head over there," Denz said.

"Should I come with you? I need to get my Jeep."

He lifted his phone from the cushion and looked at the face.

"It's early. Maybe you should try to get some more sleep?"

"Denz? What are you… Claire, what's going on in here?"

For such a big guy, her father hadn't made any noise as he'd come down the hall, but Claire could tell exactly what he was thinking when he spotted her in the same clothes as she'd worn the day before and Denz sitting all rumpled on the couch.

Denz shoved himself to his feet and quickly explained what had happened with Marsali, and once the surprise wore off, her father moved to Claire's side and hugged her.

"I'm okay, Dad." She wasn't okay that he'd obviously thought the worst of them first, but she supposed if it was Tommy and a girl in the same scenario, she'd have her rush-to-judgment doubts, too.

"Of course you are," her father said gruffly. "But one of you should've woken me up and filled me in."

"Nothing you could've done. I stayed to keep an eye on Claire while she came down from the adrenaline rush."

Claire met Denz's gaze and quickly looked away, very self-conscious of her behavior last night. "Denz was nice enough to sit with me."

Her father patted her back roughly and thanked Denz again.

"Okay, so, I'm meeting with Oliver this morning about security," he said to Tom, "but I'll take Claire's keys and bring the Jeep back with me. I shouldn't be more than a couple of hours at most, and we can get a taxi back to the wedding and drive the rental home later."

"Yeah, okay. That works." She wasn't in the right frame of mind to go and be sociable and had simply wanted to retrieve her vehicle, but Denz's plan worked fine. Eliza's crew would be there setting up, the girls would be off to the salon for hair and makeup since they were V's matron of honor and bridesmaids, and she probably wasn't awake enough to be safe behind the wheel. "I would like to see Tommy when he gets up."

Her panic over Tommy's well-being had something happened to her surged to the forefront of her mind, and she found herself struggling to breathe.

Of course, Tommy would have her father, but what if something happened to him? The potential for random disaster seemed a little more real after last night, and she felt the need for a contingency plan.

She needed people in her life. People who loved her and Tommy and would make sure that Tommy was okay if something like last night ever happened again.

It was definitely something to ponder—and another reason to follow through on Marsali's offer of matching her up.

———

IT WAS a beautiful day for a wedding. Not too hot, breezy, a perfect cloud-dotted sky that gave periodic breaks from the beaming sun.

Claire gazed at the event, awestruck by the beauty Eliza had created in the gorgeously landscaped backyards shared by the group of friends. The ceremony had taken place behind Mac's home on a terraced brick patio beneath an open gazebo. The bride's father had walked her through the circular arrangement of chairs rounding to the patio, giving every guest the perfect view of the beautiful bride and the Intercoastal behind the couple as they exchanged their vows.

A billowing tent had been placed in Carter and Eliza's

yard with lounges and chairs and other glamorous sitting areas scattered throughout.

Due to the construction still taking place at Oliver and Marsali's new home, a line of hedges had been placed to create a barrier to keep anyone from wandering that way, and if that didn't work, the extra security hired after last night's incident worked, too.

"Pretty amazing, isn't it?" Marsali asked. "No matter how large or small, Eliza never fails to dazzle."

Claire turned her attention to Marsali, who'd acted as V's matron of honor. "It's unbelievably beautiful."

"She is an artist at what she does," Marsali said. "So, how are you?"

"I think I should be asking you that. Were you able to sleep last night?"

Marsali turned her beautifully coiffed head toward her husband, who stood nearby talking to Mac, and nodded. "It took a while but I did. Oliver held me all night so I'd feel safe, but I think it was for his benefit as well. He's upset that it happened and blames himself, even though he shouldn't."

The image of Denz holding her filled her mind, and Claire felt a flush crawl up her neck.

"You know," Marsali said, "some women might not appreciate a man taking charge and being all protective, but I do."

Claire nodded her agreement silently. Credit needed to be given when it was due, and she appreciated the quality as much as Marsali.

"Denz seemed to be a comforting presence to you last night before you left," Marsali continued. "Are you sure there's nothing between you?"

"There can't be."

"Why do you say that?"

"The danger of his job, the way he travels—I don't want to be with someone like that again."

"Ah," Marsali said softly. "Well, I understand the thought process but—I still get the feeling there's more between you than just friendship."

Marsali's gaze narrowed on her, and Claire knew her expression gave her thoughts away. "I was…held last night, too."

Marsali's eyes widened and Claire shook her head. "Nothing happened. He just held me. On the couch, in the living room. All night. Because I needed it a-and asked him to."

"I see."

"I had adrenaline shakes and they *wouldn't* stop and… It was all very innocent."

"I believe you."

Claire gripped her glass so tight she was afraid it would shatter, so she set it on the railing where she stood. "Denz… He's nice. Okay? I see it. He's… He's great. But he's temporary and as soon as he passes his physical, he'll be reassigned. It would be a mistake to get close to him."

"Maybe. Or…maybe you're looking at this all wrong," Marsali said.

"What do you mean?"

"Claire, you're obviously nervous about dating again, but just as obvious is the fact you and Denz share…*something.* An attraction or curiosity or interest. Whatever you want to call it, why not use his time here to explore that?"

"Marsali, I know I had a baby at seventeen, but I'm not the type to sleep with someone when I know they're not going to stick around."

"I didn't mean that at all. Do you have my dating book? If so, you'd know that's not how I think relationships should be handled."

"It could never *be* a relationship. That's just it."

"Friendship is a relationship, Claire. And so long as Denz knows your boundaries and he's okay with them, why not use his temporary status to test the waters? Use it to get comfortable going out again, being with someone other than your husband. Practice your flirting? In that regard, Denz's temporary status is *perfect*, especially when you're already so comfortable with him. He's…safe."

Claire blinked at her beautiful friend's tantalizing suggestions and realized Marsali had a point.

Even Scott had been right to some extent, because if last night had shown her anything, it's that one just never knew what could happen, and she needed to live in the moment more than she did. Appreciate it more.

She and Denz shared…something. Like Marsali said, there was definitely a level of comfort and ease with him that Claire wasn't sure how to explain. Maybe she should do what Marsali suggested, teach herself to be in the moment with a nice man? "How do I talk to him about this? Bring it up? I don't want him to feel used, especially when there won't be side benefits," she said, making a face.

Marsali laughed softly and wrapped an arm around Claire's shoulders, turning her so that they faced Denz and Oliver and Lincoln, all three men rocking their wedding attire and looking like something from a photo shoot.

"Just let it happen naturally," Marsali said, urging Claire toward them. "Ask him to dance."

Denz's gaze locked on hers, and Claire managed to paste on a smile as they joined the men. She wet her lips and glanced up at Marsali before shifting her attention back to Denz and holding out her hand. "Dance with me?"

Chapter 20

Denz wasn't sure what had changed with Claire but something had. As one song blended into two, he tugged her closer and let his lips brush her temple. "How many glasses of champagne have you had?"

A laugh bubbled out of her, drawing a smile from him because of the sound.

"Not enough. Not to ask what I want to ask, anyway."

He drew back so that he could look into her eyes. "What's going on?"

She closed her eyes and glanced away. "Nothing. It's nothing. Forget it."

"Claire."

"It's…just something Marsali said."

"Which was?" Claire had worn the dress she'd been given by the production company after the shoot with Oliver, only this time she also wore the killer heels that left her almost eye to eye with him. Undoubtedly hurt her feet, but he'd spent the entire afternoon trying to keep his mind on whatever conversation he was in because a shift of her feet would cause the slits on the sides of the dress to expose her beautiful legs and the ridiculous shoes he found so sexy.

"She…might have pointed out that I might have been looking at your temporary status in town the wrong way, and you'd actually be a good…"

He waited for her to finish her sentence. "A good?"

"Experiment. No! That's not the right word. Oh, I'm botching this," she said, ducking her head and stepping away.

He tightened his grip and pulled her back, keeping them moving. "What kind of experiment?" Marsali's announcement last night that Claire had agreed to be matched sounded in his head, but whatever it was she hinted at, he wanted it spelled out in no uncertain terms. "Something to do with dating?"

He knew he'd guessed correctly when her nose wrinkled.

"Yeah? Like a-a practice project because we…seem to be comfortable with each other. It's probably because of the kiss scene on set a-and because you're in the garage apartment and helping with Tommy, but I-I might have told Marsali that you held me last night and it made me feel safe, and *she said*… Oh, forget it."

"Not gonna happen, sweetheart," he murmured. "Keep talking. I'm listening."

"But it's stupid. Crazy," she added. "And it's totally unfair to you because it wouldn't go anywhere. I mean, it wouldn't go *there* and most guys *expect* things to happen, but with you leaving it definitely *wouldn't*, because I'm not that… I mean, I have to have an emotional connection and… Stop smiling like that," she ordered, her eyebrows pinched over her nose.

He couldn't stop the chuckle that emerged due to her

rambling or her expression. "You do realize I wouldn't expect anything from you that you weren't willing to give."

"You say that but…it's a bad idea," she said with a shake of her blond head. "It's a bad idea, right? I wouldn't want to use you that way."

Oh, he could think of a lot of ways he wouldn't mind her using him for practice. "I think it could be fun," he said, trying and failing to hide the way they collided a bit when she stopped so abruptly.

"You do?"

"Well," he said, steering her off the dance floor to a shadowy area along the walkway. Eliza had placed over-sized lanterns filled with crystals, seashells, and flickering fake candles near a stone bench, and he led Claire that way. "You can't deny we share some chemistry, and I wouldn't mind spending the rest of my time here in town in a beautiful woman's company."

"You could go into any bar and ask any woman and she would say yes."

"So say yes," he said. "And let's have some fun."

She turned toward him as they neared the bench, her hands clasped in front of her. "Denz…"

"I can see why Marsali says you need the practice."

Claire looked insulted.

"What does that mean?"

"You're taking what will be some outings and dinners and time spent hanging out and putting a lot of unnecessary pressure on it."

"Because it's temporary, and knowing that means I'm not in danger of catching feelings for you because…I know you're leaving." The frown cleared from her face and a laugh emerged. "Oh, my gosh, you're right. I hear it. Okay. Yeah. I definitely need help, don't I?"

No danger of catching feelings for him? "Yeah, but you'd be fine."

"And you'd be okay? You wouldn't feel used?"

"You do realize I'd get to date you, right?" His gaze narrowed on her. "It's not exactly a hardship."

Her teeth sank into her lower lip and she managed a smile.

"So is it official?" he asked. "Are we dating?"

Claire stepped in front of him and stopped him in his tracks, hands gripping his waist as she leaned toward him. "I think we are. Now what?"

He grinned at her and lifted his hands to cradle her face. "Now this."

Denz brushed his lips over hers and held, just touching. He liked the way her breath hitched in her throat and felt her fingers clench into his shirt at his stomach.

He deepened the kiss, and by the time he lifted his head, he was pleased to note she looked more than a little dazed.

Yeah, kissing her wasn't going to be a hardship, either, and he planned to do plenty of it. Well, at least as much as she'd allow.

By the time he lifted his head the second time, she looked thoroughly kissed and more than a little dazed, and he felt a kick of satisfaction at the sight. "Come on, you. Let's go get some cake."

THE REST of the wedding was uneventful. Denz and Claire danced and ate cake and sipped champagne as the sun sank deeper in the sky. The day wound down and guests began to trickle away in pairs or groups, and Denz watched as the headset-wearing Eliza did her thing and began to direct catering and the cleanup crews.

Oliver had pulled Denz aside again to discuss more security ideas, and Denz promised to work on a comprehensive plan that would cover all the bases. Oliver was worried about Marsali's close call, and Denz knew the man would want nothing left to chance.

According to police, the guy's motive for being in the house was anger. The guy's girlfriend had ended things between them, and he blamed Marsali because the girlfriend had been reading Marsali's book. It just proved one never knew how someone else's mind worked. Or how freaky things could get when it came to domestic relationships.

A round of feminine laughter sounded, drawing his attention to where Claire sat with Amelia, Marsali, and Amelia's friend, Izzy. Claire held Amelia and Lincoln's baby and Denz frowned at the sight.

Claire had gotten pregnant young but she was only thirty. Did she want more kids?

A flash of jealousy stabbed him when he thought of her carrying a baby. With another guy.

"You're looking downright moody," Carter said, coming up to stand beside Denz. "What's up?"

"Nothing."

"Yeah. Keep saying that," Carter said. "This have anything to do with Claire's announcement that she's agreed to let Marsali match her up?"

Truthfully, it did. Because in the time since he'd agreed to Claire's suggestion to "test the waters" of dating, he'd found himself not liking the idea because of what would happen *after* he left town. Done right, it meant he basically wrapped Claire up in a bow and handed her off to some lucky guy from Marsali's database. And while Marsali vetted all of her clients with background checks, those didn't weed everything out, and Denz hated the idea that someone would slip through the system and not treat Claire right.

"Ah, man. You've got it bad," Carter said, clapping a hand hard on Denz's good shoulder.

"She's different," he said simply. Because it was true. Claire wasn't like the single women he'd dated. Those women were typically more into their jobs or themselves. Claire… She had a son, had a life, plans and goals. Boundaries. And he liked that about her. Respected that about her.

"The good ones always are, buddy. The good ones always are."

CLAIRE ALLOWED Denz to help her out of the SUV. He tucked her hand in his for the walk toward the door, and between her aching feet and the extra glasses of champagne she'd had with the girls before leaving, she was a little wobbly.

They made it to the porch and she giggled when she stumbled on the stairs.

"You okay there, bubbles?"

"Bubbles? Oh, the bubbly. Yup, feeling fine."

"You look it," he said, a smile in his voice. "Come on, up you go."

She gasped when the arm he had wrapped around her waist tightened and he simply lifted her up and carried her to the porch before setting her down again. "You're very strong."

"You're very cute."

"You're sweet."

Denz shifted her until her back pressed against the screen door, and he pressed against her front.

"You think I'm sweet?"

The look on his face in the dim light of the porch was anything but sweet. "And sexy."

His eyes sparkled as he stared at her.

"Right back at you, sweetheart."

Claire watched as he lowered his head. She closed her eyes and lifted her face, welcoming the kiss. Her head whirled from the sensation, and while she wanted to blame the champagne, she knew it wasn't entirely to blame.

No, it was Denz. Ever since their talk, he'd stayed by her side and showered her with attention. He'd fetched her cake and even fed her bites of his. He'd danced with her, teased her, touched her neck and the soft lobe of her ear, his big hands at her waist or the small of her back or perched along her chair.

Denz ended the kisses and lifted his head, and she saw the desire in his gaze that he didn't try to hide.

"Sweet dreams, Bubbles."

"G-good night."

He took her keys and unlocked the door before handing them back to her. She went inside and locked the door behind her, then moved to the kitchen sink to look out the window.

Denz stayed on the porch for a long moment before turning and heading toward the garage.

Claire watched him go, wishing she was brave enough to follow.

Chapter 21

Ten days later, Claire donned her bathing suit and finished packing her beach bag for a day on the water. She was insanely nervous about going out with Denz in such a public way, but Oliver had invited Denz and Claire to join in on the fun, and Claire knew Marsali was behind the invitation.

Ever since the wedding, she and Denz had spent every spare moment of time together. They went to the beach to sun or to walk, out to eat, to the movies. They went on a dinner cruise on the Cape Fear River, took the ferry to Bald Head Island and spent the day riding from beach to beach on a golf cart, and checked out several restaurants and music groups downtown.

They cooked out with Tommy and her father, rode bikes through the neighborhood, and had ice cream on the swings by the pier. Every day held a new adventure of some sort, and even though some of the time was spent doing mundane things, like washing her Jeep after taking it out on the sand, it was still special and fun due to the man she was with.

Claire left her bedroom and moved through the house to find Tommy waiting in the living room. "Wow. You beat me." Here she thought she'd have to prod him along.

"I didn't want to make you late. Is it a big boat? How many Jet Skis do they have? Where are we going?"

She smiled at the barrage of questions and shook her head. "You know as much as I do. I guess we'll find out when we get there."

"And they're okay with me coming, too?"

"Denz invited us both." Apparently that wasn't the thing to say, because Tommy's excited expression changed to a frown.

"Mom, are you dating him?"

Tommy had hung out with his new friends a lot this week and even attended a birthday party for one of the kids, but Claire knew she couldn't hide anything from him, especially when they all lived in such close quarters. "We're friends, Tommy. That hasn't changed."

"But he likes you."

"What?"

Tommy crossed his arms over his chest and looked very much like his father when he stared at her.

"Denz told me he likes you but you needed more than a friend and he wasn't that guy."

"When was this?" she asked, lowering her bag to the couch to give herself something to focus on instead of the jab of unease currently pummeling her stomach.

"One day when we were driving to the gym."

"What else did he say?"

"He said he wasn't going to tell you how he felt because he would be leaving soon, but I heard you tell Marsali you weren't going to work as much this week. Is it so you can go out with him?"

Oh, how she hated old houses and thin walls. "Tommy,

Denz and I are *friends*, but… Yes, we've decided to hang out together while he's in town. It's nothing serious and nothing you need to worry about."

"So you don't like him?"

That again? "I like him *as a friend*. Otherwise I wouldn't want to spend time with him. But it's not serious, because like you said, Denz will be leaving and… It's like your new friends at the gym. You said there are girls in the weightlifting group, and you all hang out together on the beach. Denz and I are spending time together so we don't have to do things alone, and having fun. That's all."

"I just don't want you to get hurt, Mom."

Her heart pinched at his grown-up words, and she moved toward him, wrapping him in a hug, amazed as always when he lowered his head atop hers. When had her little boy gotten so big? "Thank you for watching out for me." She squeezed him. "You know, I've been thinking. I may have overreacted when I added a full month to your punishment." She leaned her head back to look at him. "So I'm going to let you off with time served. You can have it back so long as you stay out of trouble."

"Really?"

"When we get back," she quickly added. "You can't take it on the boat and you can't stay home to play it."

"Thanks, Mom. And I'll stay out of trouble. I promise."

Claire laughed when he picked her up off her feet and then set her down again. "Just be the young man I know you can be."

"Mom?"

"Yeah?"

"It's okay if you like Denz. I mean, he seems nice."

"That's…surprising."

Tommy shrugged. "I've just been thinking, is all. My

friend Madison's mom died six months ago, and she said her dad is already engaged."

"Oh."

"Yeah. I get you being lonely, though. Dad was gone almost two years before he was killed, so even though it's only been a year, it probably feels like more to you. I didn't think about that before."

Claire stared into Tommy's gaze and patted his cheek. "And you don't need to think about it now. Stop worrying about me and let's go have some fun, okay?"

"Okay."

She told Tommy to get the cooler she'd packed for them and gathered up her bag once more.

She wasn't sure whether she should be thankful for Madison's dad and his engagement, but she was thankful it had made Tommy think beyond himself. Coming to Carolina Cove had been good for him, and she prayed it would be an easy transition once they lived here full-time and he started school. It certainly seemed this set of friends was better for him than the ones back in Virginia.

Claire ran through the list she'd made on her phone. She wasn't sure what to bring other than towels, sunscreen, lip balm, and the like, but she'd tossed in a few other items just in case. Earphones seemed to be rude when on a boat with other people, but she grabbed a set for Tommy in case he got bored with the adults.

She checked her watch and headed for the door, spotting Denz descending from the apartment. He hadn't worn his shoulder sling since before the wedding, yet another sign of his healing and the fact he would be leaving sooner rather than later. He'd continued with his PT and she knew he was making progress.

"Hey, you. Good morning."

"Morning," she said. "I hope we didn't keep you waiting?"

"Not at all. Got everything you need?" he asked, unlocking his SUV and tossing a backpack into the rear compartment.

"I think so. I packed a cooler for us, just in case."

"I'm sure they'll have plenty but it's a nice gesture. Tommy, you ready for some fun?"

TWENTY MINUTES LATER, they were on the boat and heading up the Intercoastal toward Masonboro Island. The guys were gathered around Lincoln as he captained them, Tommy included, and Claire was thankful that the men were making an effort to include her son in the conversation. Lincoln's son from his first marriage had joined them today as well, and though he was eighteen and in college, Claire noticed he shared a love of music and games with Tommy, and the two talked freely.

"Tommy is fine. Stop staring," Marsali said.

"Sorry. Can't help it." The ladies sat on the lower level, sunning themselves as the boat trolled along the waterway.

"I wish Breanne would've come today but she said she'd rather babysit," Amelia added. "She's saving up for a trip to New York City with her friends and is more interested in earning money than a day on the water."

"Good for her. A trip sounds like a great goal. Cute suit, Claire," Eliza said. "I like that."

"Thanks. Yours, too," Claire said, smiling.

"So?" Marsali asked, leaning toward Claire. "How's things going?"

Claire laughed at the question. "I'm good."

"You know that's not what I'm asking," Marsali said. "I

saw you and Denz kissing quite a bit at the wedding and you've been quietly MIA since."

"Wait, what?" Eliza asked. "How did I miss that?"

"You were busy," Marsali said to her friend.

"I noticed, too," Amelia added, tilting her head to one side. "Looked to be as hot as the kisses you shared on camera."

Claire took the teasing in stride and simply shook her head and pulled her floppy hat from the bag beside her. "We're friends."

"Kissing friends," Marsali added. "Oliver has tracked with Denz this whole time because of the security project, and you've been a busy girl with all of those dates."

"We're…having fun," Claire said, fixing the brim so that it shaded her eyes.

"What's that mean?" Eliza asked.

"It means we're spending time together while he's in town," she told them, "but we're just friends."

"Can men and women be friends?" Eliza asked. "I've never known that to be true. It seems like one or the other always develops feelings."

"Well, either way, he's not been entirely friend-zoned," Amelia added with a smile.

"Can we talk about something else?" Claire asked, feeling more than a little self-conscious.

"Things are going well, though?" Marsali asked. "Just tell us that and we'll drop it. For now."

Claire thought of all the dates and fun and kissing she'd shared and nodded. "Things are going very well."

She didn't want to think about the time when Denz would leave town, so she forced herself to compartmentalize that to be dealt with later. She was on a mission to live in the moment, one moment at a time.

The boat slowed and Claire looked around to find

they'd come to an isolated stretch of the uninhabited island.

"Just remember," Marsali said, her voice low because the men were heading down the stairs toward them, "we're here for you."

Claire felt Denz's gaze on her and looked his way. He'd removed his shirt, and his broad chest and muscled abs were marred only by the scars on his shoulder. The bruising had faded since their first meeting, but the bullet-sized scar was a huge reminder of why Claire couldn't allow herself to plan beyond the moment.

She'd decided she would never again be with someone who got shot at for a living. And for all his kindness and good looks and chemistry, Denz didn't even allow his father to be contacted unless he was critical—dying.

And if that wasn't a red flag for a big ol' never again, she didn't know what was.

Chapter 22

Denz stared at Claire floating in the water and wondered how she'd gotten under his skin so easily. The time they'd spent together had been fun, and he'd found himself picturing them as more. Like they were a real couple who lived locally, just going about their daily lives. Holding hands as they went to dinner or walked on the boardwalk by the pier.

He moved into the water and headed her way. Swimming arm over arm without a twinge of pain.

He hated the news he had to share with her, because it would wipe the smile from her beautiful face, but he knew he couldn't put it off any longer.

He made it to where she was and wrapped his arm around her waist, floating her toward him. "Hey, you."

Her back met his chest and he dropped a kiss to her salty shoulder in the shallow water.

"Hey."

"Having fun?"

She turned to face him, her arms pushing against him so that she wasn't so close.

"Yeah."

"Claire? You okay?"

"I'm fine. You?"

Okay, something was definitely wrong. "You don't want me to touch you?"

"No, it's not… It's just Tommy is here and everyone is watching us. I feel like we're under a microscope."

He supposed that was a consideration. "Were the girls grilling you on our relationship?"

"And then some. It's…awkward."

He knew the anger he felt wasn't justified, but he wanted her not to care that he was who he was, or what her friends thought. "You know, we could always do long-distance."

She blinked her spiky wet eyelashes at his statement. "What?"

"When I get reassigned. I get days off. You could fly out and visit me, or we could meet up somewhere halfway."

"Denz… I have a child. I'll have a job—I'm selling my house and moving. I can't…"

"Yeah. Yeah, of course. It was just a thought because you said… Forget I mentioned it."

"I'm glad you did, it's just that I can't."

"I know. I'm going in."

"Denz—"

He swam toward the shore and made his way to the towel spread out on the hot sand. They'd anchored the boat a ways out, and right now Carter took Tommy out on the Jet Ski, Marsali and Oliver swam, and the others walked the island, shell hunting.

Water droplets hit him, and he opened his eyes to find Claire dropping down beside him on her stomach.

"Please don't be upset," she said softly. "But I said from

the beginning that I couldn't handle your job. You know that about me, and once you go back and do what you do—"

"I know. It's okay." Except it wasn't. At some point, he'd started to care for Claire as more than a friend, and he'd like to see where their relationship could go, but when she wouldn't even consider an attempt at compromise…

"Denz, I have Tommy to consider. He's already lost his father. I've already lost a husband. And then there's the fact that…I've basically been a single parent most of Tommy's life, and at that time, I signed up for it as a military spouse. But next time—when there is a next time—I don't want that to be the case. I want a relationship and a co-parent and dinners together at the table."

"And that's not something I can give you," he said honestly. "Not regularly. I get it. I'm sorry, Claire."

"Yeah. Me, too."

He inhaled and rolled onto his side, propping his head up on his hand while he took in the sight of her, belly-down on the towel beside him. "This is lousy timing but…I passed my physical yesterday. I'm waiting on reassignment."

Had he not been watching her, he would've missed the way her entire body tensed. Her head was turned toward him but her eyes were closed. He reached out and stroked his fingertips down her arm, brushing the sand and water droplets away. "I should hear something any minute."

"Okay. Thanks f-for telling me."

Her voice sounded low, thready and thick with a hint of tears.

He rolled onto his back and stared up at the blue sky overhead, the sound of the surf and the buzz of Jet Skis doing nothing to disguise the sniffle Claire couldn't hide.

DENZ RECEIVED news regarding his new assignment that evening.

They'd returned from their outing and had just docked at the marina when his phone rang, and his expression told Claire exactly who it was and why they were calling.

Denz walked away to talk privately while she and Tommy grabbed their bags and unloaded like everyone else. Carter helped her off the boat, and everyone stood somewhat awkwardly waiting on Denz to rejoin them.

"Claire?" Marsali asked. "You okay?"

"Fine." She felt Tommy's gaze on her and forced a smile. "Hey, what are we eating tonight? All the fresh air and swimming has left me hungry."

Tommy shrugged. "I don't care."

"We could all meet at Reels for dinner," Marsali said. "Mac and V will be there since they just got back from their honeymoon."

"I was thinking more along the lines of fast food on the way home to shower off the salt and sand," Claire said. "Thanks, though."

"Yessir," Denz said, his voice carrying on the breeze.

"Oh. That sounds official," Eliza said with a grimace.

"He passed his physical," Claire announced. "It's… probably his new assignment."

"So soon?" Marsali asked.

Denz turned and headed their way and everyone watched his approach.

"Well? Where are you heading off to?" Claire said, forcing a lightness to the words and a brave face.

Denz shoved his sunglasses atop his head as he joined them.

"Miami. Tomorrow afternoon."

She'd promised her father she would work tomorrow because his regular guy needed a day off for a funeral. Maybe it was best.

Claire murmured goodbye to the group and hugged the girls before she turned and headed toward the parking area.

"Do you have to go?" Tommy asked from behind her.

Claire kept walking, her heart in her throat as she eavesdropped on them.

"Yeah, bud. I'm sorry. Orders are orders."

"You're not in the military, though. Tell them you can't go."

"It's my job, Tommy. I have to go where I'm needed."

She yanked on the door handle only to discover it still locked and fought the urge to stomp her foot in frustration. She turned her back to them and waited impatiently on the beep.

The moment it sounded, she grabbed at the door again and Denz's hand closed over hers.

"I'm sorry, Claire," he said softly.

She nodded. Because what else could she do? It wasn't like she hadn't known from the beginning that it would never be more than temporary. "Take me home, please."

The trip to her father's house was made in total silence. Denz didn't even turn on the radio as he made the turns and finally pulled into the driveway.

Tommy bolted before the vehicle had fully stopped, and Claire felt like doing the same, though she sat there while Denz shut off the engine and turned toward her.

"Claire."

She surged across the seat toward him and pressed her lips to his, silencing whatever platitudes he was about to make. She didn't want to hear them. Couldn't. Because she was already pulled so taut she felt like her body would break from the tension.

So she kissed him. Kissed him like it was the last time, because it was and it sucked and she might never see him again. Because her heart was breaking and they'd barely had any time together and yet she couldn't stop from feeling what she felt.

The kiss was gritty and salty, heat and sadness, full of bittersweet desperation for what might have been. And when it was over and she pulled away, she stared at his handsome face, searing it into her brain. "Stay safe."

"Claire."

"Stay *safe*," she whispered. "Goodbye, Marcus."

"Claire."

"What? Do you want me to ask you to stay? I won't. I *can't*. You either want to or you don't. You either choose to stay o-or you *don't,* but it has to be your choice because you know that I can't... Your job... People shooting at you? Just...promise me you'll stay safe."

He didn't speak and she knew why. Denz didn't break his promises and his safety wasn't in his control. Wasn't up to him but whoever he came up against in the name of protecting someone else.

Claire got out and raced for the house. Thankfully her father wasn't in sight, and she ignored Tommy's closed door and quickly grabbed a change of clothes before heading to the shower. She stayed there under the water until it turned cold and then emerged to find multiple messages from Marsali and Eliza. She ignored them and knocked on Tommy's door. When he didn't answer, she opened it to find him in bed. "Hey. You okay?"

"He's going to die," her son whispered softly. "Just like Dad."

The words were so thick with emotion she could barely make them out.

Her heart broke all over again, and she entered the room and sat on the edge of his bed to rub her hand over his back. "He'll be careful."

"He was already shot."

"It's his life, Tommy."

"But what about you? Don't you get a say?"

She blinked hard and tried to find the words. "It's not like that. It never was. There are certain decisions we have to make on our own, and this is one of them for Denz. He has to choose because otherwise he would resent us."

"Why didn't Dad choose us? Why did he keep going back?"

She'd asked herself that question many times over the years. Especially after he'd been wounded on his second tour and chose to go back a third time. "Dad always told me he had to. That's all I know. He felt it was his duty to his country and to his men."

Tommy turned his face into the pillow and sobbed. "I hate them. I hate them both."

Claire leaned over him and hugged him, her cheek pressed against his hot back. "You don't mean that. It wouldn't hurt so much if you hated them. You love them both."

Just like I do.

Chapter 23

The next day, Claire stared dazedly at the hamburgers frying on the grill inside the craft service van and tried not to let her thoughts drift to Denz.

When she'd woken up this morning and looked out the kitchen window, his rental was gone and the bag carrying Tommy's game system was on the kitchen table.

Her father had already made coffee, and he'd given her a hard stare as he'd told her Denz had brought it over before saying goodbye.

She'd nodded and got her coffee, trying hard to pretend the news hadn't gutted her. She wasn't sure what she expected after the scene in the car when he'd driven them back from the marina, but she'd be lying if she pretended a part of her hadn't hoped to wake up this morning with Denz on the doorstep because he'd decided to stay.

"You!"

Claire startled so badly at the loud voice she dropped the spatula she held. It clattered as it bounced off the grill onto the floor.

The woman who'd come to the van before to get Claire to be a stand-in hurried through the narrow space to grab Claire by the elbow.

"We need you again. Right now."

"I'm working."

The woman lowered her chin to her chest and shot Claire a look over the top of her black-rimmed glasses.

"We need you."

"Claire, go. It's fine," her father said. "Tommy and I can handle things."

Tommy was in as bad shape as she was today, unable to focus and having to redo things. "Dad, are you sure?"

"Go," Tom said. "Just make sure she gets paid," he said to the woman.

"Oh, she'll be fine," the woman said. "Now come on. We have to hurry."

The woman prodded Claire out of the van and down the blocked street into a building.

"Here. Put this on," the woman said.

Claire looked at the black turtleneck, black leggings, and black booties and frowned. "Who am I supposed to be this time?"

"Jewel thief. Hurry up."

Claire rushed to change, pulling on the hot clothes, all the while hoping the set was air conditioned.

Once dressed, she was shoved into a chair and her makeup quickly done. She'd French braided her today due to the heat and dealing with food, and other than a quick touch-up of a curling iron to the tendrils around her face, her braids were left alone.

Deemed ready, she followed the woman, who led her to a set decorated to look like an interrogation room.

"Sit and hold out your hands."

Amelia stepped forward from out of the shadows and smiled at Claire.

"Hey, you."

"Hi."

Amelia clicked handcuffs together and smiled. "Don't worry, I have the key."

Claire blinked. "Those are for me?"

"Yup," Amelia said, fastening one to Claire's wrist before fixing the links to the table and clicking the cuffs on Claire's other hand.

"Okay, guys, let's get this done. Claire, thanks for helping us out again," Oliver said, walking toward her.

"Um, sure. Where's the actress?"

"She has a migraine, but we need to run through this scene and make sure we get the lighting and sound right."

"I have to *speak*?"

"Just ad-lib."

Ad-lib? "But what do I say?"

"You'll be fine. Just wing it," he said, moving behind the cameras to take a seat.

Wing it? *Wing it?*

"The setup is you're a jewel thief. You've been caught after stashing the goods, and you're about to face the head of security."

That's it? That's all the information she got? How was she supposed to—

"Action!"

She startled at the shout and then again at the clap of the marker thing in front of her face.

A door opened behind her but she faced the wrong way. She sat there, hands cuffed to the table, light shining down on her from overhead, and waited for the other person to speak.

"You thought you'd get away with it, didn't you?"

Denz?

She turned and squinted into the darkened corner but wasn't able to make him out for certain. "Get away with wh-what?"

He stepped closer, into the light, and she gasped when she saw that it really was Denz.

He was there? But…Miami.

"The moment I laid eyes on you, I knew you were trouble."

She didn't respond. Wasn't sure how to respond. What was happening? Her father had said Denz had a flight out of Wilmington that morning but—

"And you," Denz said, slowly strolling around the table until he faced her. "You thought you'd get away with it."

"Get away with what? You have no proof," she said, remembering Oliver's statement about ad-libbing and stashing the goods.

"That's where you're wrong. I let you take it, you know."

"I don't know what you're talking about," she said.

Denz placed his hands on the table and leaned toward her, and she stared into his mahogany gaze.

"You got close to me, used me, because you thought I was safe—temporary."

Wait, what? Was that in the script she didn't have?

"But what if I wasn't?"

She blinked at him and swallowed hard. "Wasn't…what?"

"Temporary. What if," he drawled, seating himself on the edge of the table facing her, "you found out I was just a regular guy, working a regular job—here."

Claire blinked, so confused because she wanted to believe this was more than a scene for Oliver to check his lighting and sound and yet…too afraid to believe in more.

What was Denz doing? Had he taken up acting? What part of this was real and what wasn't? "What crime did I commit…exactly?"

Denz leaned toward her even more, not stopping until their noses almost touched.

"You stole my heart," he said softly.

The air left her lungs in a huff, and Claire wet her lips, wishing they didn't have an audience. "I… I suppose it's only fair."

"Because?"

"You stole mine."

Denz's gaze narrowed on her, and he shoved himself up and moved around the table until he stood behind her.

"You didn't answer the question," he said. "What if I was *that* guy? One who finally decided to put down roots. Would it make a difference?"

A regular guy with a regular job? It sounded heavenly. "It might," she said, trying to play off the words as casually as possible.

"I need more than that, sweetheart."

"It would," she said, cheeks heating because she was literally chained to a table with an audience while they talked.

"Are you sure? Because you don't date. You told me yourself…after you admitted to not reading your friend's dating book."

A sharp "Ha! I *knew* it," sounded from behind the scenes, and Claire recognized the voice as belonging to Marsali.

Soft laughter filled the area, and Claire bit back an embarrassed smile and shook her head. She'd have to apologize to Marsali later. "I didn't read it because I didn't think I was ready to date."

"What about now?"

What about now? Was this really happening? "F-for the right guy, yes. I-I mean, if I met *that* guy, I'd have no excuse or reason not to…see where things might go. Are you going to uncuff me?"

"I'm a by-the-book kind of guy. Regulations state the cuffs stay on until you confess. Do you confess?"

She smiled and shrugged. "Only if you confess first."

From their audience, she heard someone say, "*Thatta girl.*"

Denz braced one hand on the table beside her, one on the back of her chair, and leaned close enough that she smelled his cologne and a hint of soap and coffee.

"I confess I like you, Claire Simmons. Enough to jump at a job offer and stick around because you…you make me want to. Now, are you going to date me or not?" he asked, the words whispered softly near her ear.

"Mmm."

"That's not an answer."

"Actually, it is."

"How so?"

"Because I think I already am."

"Cut!"

OCTOBER SUNSETS WERE spectacular in Carolina Cove, and as Claire stared out at the water near Marsali's home, she thanked God for the beauty He'd gifted them with for their special day.

The last four and a half months had held a lot of changes. She'd sold the Virginia house and moved, gotten Tommy settled in school. Fallen head over heels in love and started a business as a virtual assistant.

Claire turned and spotted her father as he approached

her from across the yard. Two hours ago, she'd accepted his arm for the walk down the aisle to where Denz and Tommy waited, both tall and handsome in their suits.

She hadn't been able to look away from her gorgeous fiancé—Oliver's new head of security—as she'd moved past the small group of friends gathered behind Oliver and Marsali's new home.

Her new home.

Due to Denz's new position, Oliver had offered to sell the small guest house at the end of the street as part of Denz's employment package. After all, it couldn't hurt to have someone like Denz actually living next door.

Denz's comprehensive security plan and Oliver's job offer had led Denz to create his own security firm. His company now handled security for all of Oliver's film ventures as well as their personal security in Carolina Cove, plus a rapidly growing list of clients in the area.

While Denz's job still involved an element of danger, he was more businessman, logistics engineer, and coordinator than bodyguard, and he did his job exceedingly well. Especially since he knew what was involved to guard someone so closely.

Another change had been Denz contacting his father. The man had come for a visit a month ago and decided to move from Savannah to Carolina Cove. As of Friday, he lived in the apartment above her father's garage, and George and her father had become fast friends.

Her gaze shifted and settled on her son, seated at a table beside his plus-one, a pretty brunette girl from Tommy's school. Tommy had reminded her of what she'd said about no one wanting to go to a wedding alone, and that's when she'd realized her son had his first crush.

Tommy caught her watching them and smiled shyly.

Tears flooded Claire's eyes, but they were happy ones born out of a heart ready to burst because it was so full of love.

Tommy had made a huge turnaround since they'd come here. He'd settled into school, was doing great in therapy, had joined the lacrosse team, and his grades were back up. She was so proud of him, and she loved the relationship Tommy and Denz shared.

They had their "guy time" at the gym four days a week, and Denz encouraged Tommy's interest in computers due to the security aspect and job potential for cybersecurity. Tommy loved the idea and, as of now, considered it his future career.

She inhaled as her father grew closer, and used the moment to imprint the view in her mind because the yard held all of her favorite people.

Eliza had insisted on gifting Claire and Denz with her services, and when added to the beautiful backdrop, Claire felt their intimate wedding was the most breathtaking of all.

"You know, I've never seen you this happy. Ever," her father said.

She shifted her gaze and realized her big, tough father struggled to hold back tears. "I…don't think I've ever been this happy," she said, admitting that the life she'd shared before was good—but it wasn't the same as this.

It was amazing what time and maturity could do when it came to opening one's eyes.

"Well, I'm happy for you both," Tom said, giving her a hug. "You were a beautiful bride, Claire. I'm glad I got to see it this time," he said with a wink.

Music started to play and she felt Denz's presence behind her. She turned and watched him approach. "Hi, husband."

"Wife," he said with a dip of his head and a too sexy smile. "Dance with me?"

She placed her hand in his and let Denz lead her to the center of the beautiful travertine patio. He drew her into his arms and they began to sway back and forth.

"Have I told you how beautiful you look today?"

She closed her eyes and rubbed her temple against his chin, loving the feel of his skin. "Hmm. Several times. And just so you know, you clean up pretty well yourself. This day couldn't have been more perfect, could it?"

Denz stopped moving and she stared up at him, loving the love she saw in his mahogany gaze and the tender way he looked at her.

She smiled at him and rose onto her toes to press a soft kiss to his lips, relishing the moment because her tough guy struggled to express himself. "I know," she said softly, still amazed by the fact his temporary status had turned into something so permanent. "Me, too."

WANT TO READ OTHER BOOKS SET IN MY FICTIONAL COASTAL TOWN OF CAROLINA COVE? CHECK OUT AN EXCERPT OF THE LAST GOODBYE:

Dominic Dunn hit his turn signal and waited for a family of five to cross the sidewalk before he turned into the Carolina Cove Inn lot and parked, dread filling his stomach. Just the sight of the happy families and tourists wandering the sidewalks, lounging on restaurant patios, and enjoying the lively Saturday night left him angry. He should've ignored the letter. Ignored his next-door neighbor and best friend, ignored his boss and coworkers who said he had to honor Lisa's last request and come here.

"Mister? You gonna get out?"

The boy's voice startled Dominic and he turned to see

a kid around eight years old watching him. The salt-air breeze blowing through the open windows of his car brought with it the smell of fried foods from the restaurants nearby, and seagulls squawked as they flew overhead.

"Mister?"

"Yeah," Dominic said, only then realizing he'd pulled into a parking place and was literally sitting there with his foot on the brake as he debated his choices of whether to throw the new car in reverse and floor it to get out of Carolina Cove as quickly as possible… or stay the prepaid two weeks Lisa had booked for him before her death.

"Doesn't look like it. Are you drunk?"

A rough-sounding chuckle left his chest. "Do you get a lot of drunk people here?"

"Sometimes."

"I see. Well, I'm not drunk. Just trying to decide if I want to stay here."

"Oh. You got a reservation?"

Did the kid ever stop asking questions? A memory formed, that of his son, Elijah, at the same age. "Yeah, I do."

"Then why don't you wanna stay?"

Dominic glanced at the clock and noted the time. If he left now, he'd add another six hours to his drive from Atlanta. Not how he wanted to spend what was left of the day. Maybe he should spend the night and head back to Atlanta first thing in the morning? "You've convinced me. I guess I will stay."

"I'll show you the way to the office."

"Do your parents know you're out here near the street? You're awfully young to be wandering about on your own."

The kid's shoulders squared and he lifted his chin to a defiant angle.

"I'm almost ten."

He looked younger, maybe because of his small stature. "Well, almost ten or not, there are a lot of strangers milling around, and it's not safe for kids these days. Are you visiting?" He sounded like an old man talking about "the good old days" but it was true. What kind of parent just let their kid wander the streets in a beach town full of people, some of whom probably waited on the opportunity to grab a kid and head out of town?

"No. I live here. You coming or not?"

The kid had spunk, Dominic had to give him that.

He rolled up the windows of the Porsche 911, killing the powerful engine with another press of a button. He felt a little conspicuous driving the flashy car, but he had to admit he loved the power. Just like Lisa knew he would.

He opened the door and climbed out of the low vehicle, yet another thing to get used to after driving a family-friendly SUV for so many years.

"Wow. You're tall. My mom is too. I hope I'm tall when I grow up."

Dominic locked the car and fell into step behind the boy. "I see the sign for the office. You can head home if you like."

"No. I need to check in anyway." The kid turned around and walked backward, rolling his eyes in classic kid fashion. "Or my mom will freak out and call the police again."

Again? "Does that happen a lot?"

"Her calling the police or freaking out?"

"Take your pick."

"Yeah."

Yeah to… both? Dom bit back another chuckle. Given the kid's intrepid personality, he probably kept his mom busy.

The kid flipped face-forward and Dom watched as the

boy ran up the two steps leading to the office. He yanked open the door.

"Mom! Reservation!"

Dom noted the wide southern porch with its rocking chairs and a few chairs and tables before he followed the kid inside, well able to see why Lisa had liked the inn so much if the porch and office interior were anything by which to judge. It was her style of decorating. Beachy but understated.

The office walls were a soft gray with blue and sand-colored accents. There was a comfortable-looking couch and chair in the waiting area, a rope swing hanging from the ceiling in front of a painted mural of the beach and ocean behind, and on the opposite side, a coffee bar, popcorn machine, and snack area with a couple of parlor-type tables and chairs.

"Mom!"

"Samuel, how many times have I told you? No yelling. Inside voice," a woman stated as she appeared from a hallway behind the chest-high desk.

Dominic stilled, uncomfortable with the stomach-punching fact he found her beautiful. He'd guess her age to be early to mid-thirties, tall like her son said, at around five eight. Her auburn hair was scooped back and held at her nape, but curly tendrils framed her face and highlighted striking eyes that matched the blue of the ocean painting behind the check-in area.

"But, Mom, you have a reservation and sometimes don't hear me."

"A— Oh," she said, locking gazes with Dominic. "Sorry about that. Welcome to Carolina Cove Inn. I'm Ireland Cohen, the manager."

He forced himself to focus on her name rather than her beauty. "Ireland? Like the country?"

"Yes."

"Unusual name."

"Unusual family," she said by way of explanation. She flashed them both a smile. "I hope I didn't keep you waiting too long?"

"Not at all. Samuel kept me company."

"Mom, you should see his cool car! I'll bet it goes really fast. Does it?"

"It does."

"Maybe you'll take me for a ride sometime?"

"Samuel."

"I'm leaving tomorrow."

"Oh."

"And even if he wasn't, Samuel, that's not something you ask our guests. We've talked about this, remember?" the boy's mother said while sliding her son a stern glare.

"Yes, ma'am."

Samuel glanced at Dominic and rolled his eyes, and yet again Dom found himself stifling a chuckle. And wondering at the last time he'd laughed so much in such a short span of time. "Tough break, kid."

"Let's get you checked in. Name?"

"Dominic Dunn."

"Domin—"

His name ended with a gasp and Ireland's eyes filled with tears. She blinked rapidly and managed to keep them from falling, but in that instant, he knew she recognized him—and knew his reason for being there.

CLICK THE LAST GOODBYE TO KEEP READING!

MONTANA SECRETS SERIES:

- HEALING HER COWBOY
- IT HAD TO BE YOU
- HERS TO KEEP
- MILLION DOLLAR STANDOFF
- HIS CHRISTMAS WISH
- THEIR SECRET SON

THE SEASIDE SISTERS SERIES:

- THE LAST GOODBYE
- LATTES AND LULLABYES
- MAP OF DREAMS
- WORTH THE RISK
- LOST LOVE FOUND

TAMING THE TULANES SERIES:

- SMALL TOWN SCANDAL
- THEIR SECRET BARGAIN
- CROSSING THE LINE
- THE NANNY'S SECRET
- SOMEONE TO TRUST

THE STONE RIVER SERIES:

- WORTH THE WAIT
- NOT BY SIGHT
- THROUGH THE VALLEY

- LEAD ME NOT
- CHRISTMAS AT HOLLY WOOD
- THEIR CHRISTMAS MIRACLE
- SECOND CHANCES

SMALL TOWN SCANDALS SERIES:

- BRODY'S REDEMPTION
- FALLING FOR HER BOSS
- WITH THIS MAN

SECRET SANTA SERIES:

- SECRET SANTA
- SECRET SANTA II: A CHRISTMAS TO REMEMBER

MAKE ME A MATCH SERIES:

- ROMANCE RESET
- RULES OF ENGAGEMENT
- THE MATCHMAKER'S SECRET
- PERFECTLY MISMATCHED
- BY THE BOOK

FAQ

Is Carolina Cove a real place?

Carolina Cove is purely fictional; however, it is **loosely** based on one of my favorite places—Kure Beach, North Carolina. Kure Beach is home to a wonderful pier, a pavilion for special events like weddings and birthdays, swings facing the Atlantic, pelicans Pete and George, coffee shops, restaurants, and more. It's also close to the North Carolina Aquarium, Carolina Beach, and Wilmington.

Can I stay at the Carolina Cove Inn?

While Carolina Cove and the Carolina Cove Inn are purely fictional, there are plenty of motels and rentals in the area to enjoy.

But the pier is real?

Yes! And it has quite a history. Be sure to check out the Kure Beach Pier Cam for a view of Kure Beach and the Atlantic.

What about the restaurants and coffee shops and places you've mentioned in the series?

London's Lattes is based on two of my favorite local coffee shops in Kure Beach and Carolina Beach. Are there more? Yes, plenty. But those two shops I know well because I've visited fairly often while writing these stories. Neither of them on their own was perfect for what I had in mind for London's, however, so I basically combined the two and ta-da! London's Lattes was born. But, no, if you go into either of them, you won't find London's exact business. Isn't fiction wonderful?

Why make up a city? Why not use Kure Beach?

One of the best things about writing fiction is that when a story appears a certain way, you can write it just that way. Carolina Cove and the characters appeared to me in story form and while Kure Beach IS one of my favorite places, I had to change some things to better fit the series as well as steer far away from any real-life persons/families for obvious reasons. Doing so, that meant also changing the name of the city, etc. But, that said, you will find a slew of similarities in the fictional city and the real one. :)

Where is the dream catcher mailbox?

Unfortunately the dream catcher mailbox is pure fiction and an idea taken from a "beach mailbox" I visited once many years ago. The dream catcher mailbox first appeared in the SEASIDE SISTERS SERIES.

How did you research the matchmaking aspect?

Oh, the answer to this was fun! Wilmington actually has a professional matchmaker. I interviewed her to get my details straight and learned a lot about a very fascinating business!

MAKE ME A MATCH SERIES:

- ROMANCE RESET
- RULES OF ENGAGEMENT
- THE MATCHMAKER'S SECRET
- PERFECTLY MISMATCHED
- BY THE BOOK

About the Author

Kay Lyons always wanted to be a writer, ever since the age of seven or eight when she copied the pictures out of a Charlie Brown book and rewrote the story because she didn't like the plot. Through the years her stories have changed but one characteristic stayed true— they were all romances. Each and every one of her manuscripts included a love story.

Published in 2005 with Harlequin Enterprises, Kay's first release was a national bestseller. Kay has also been a HOLT Medallion, Book Buyers Best and RITA Award nominee. Look for her most recent novels with Kindred Spirits Publishing.

For more information regarding her work, please visit Kay at the following:

www.kaylyonsauthor.com

@KayLyonsAuthor (Twitter)

Kay Lyons Author (Facebook)

Author_Kay_Lyons (Instagram)

Kay Lyons, Author (Pinterest)

SIGN UP FOR KAY'S NEWSLETTER AND RECEIVE UPDATES ON NEW RELEASES, CONTESTS, PRE-RELEASE BOOK INFORMATION, EXCLUSIVES AND MORE!